KALEIDOSCOPE

KALEIDOSCOPE

JINNY ALEXANDER   ALAINE GREYSON   KJ LYONS
KYLEIGH MCCLOUD   ANDREW PARKER
LO POTTER   MIKE VANDEVENTER

Creative James Media
Copyright © 2021 Three Colors of Life by Kyleigh McCloud
Copyright © 2021 Rainbow Row by K J Lyons
Copyright © 2021 The Blue Milk Journal by Mike VandeVenter
Copyright © 2021 Living Colours by Andrew Parker
Copyright © 2021 Southern Hospitality, The Grey by Lo Potter
Copyright © 2021 The Aerialist, A Darker Shade of Pink by Jinny Alexander
Copyright © 2021 Privilege and Blue Melancholy, Fire by Alaine Greyson

ISBN: paperback: 978-1-7353926-4-6
ISBN: ebook: 978-1-7353926-7-7
Library of Congress Control Number: 2021935447

Cover Design by Diana TC, triumphcovers.com
Edited by Brian Paone
Logo by Kevin Harless
First Printing Edition 2021
Published by Creative James Media
Pasadena, MD 21122

❀ Created with Vellum

CONTENTS

THREE COLORS OF LIFE

BY KYLEIGH MCCLOUD

Golden-brown hair strands flittered around Emily's head like a crown. Overhead, the sun sparkled, its prisms filtering a rainbow within the clear water. Pretty colors. She reached for the dancing kaleidoscope spots. Bubbles escaped from her lips and floated to the surface. Tadpoles swirled around her, nibbling at her fingers and toes. Emily giggled on the inside as they tickled her exposed skin.

Ma's face shimmered above, and silent words came from her.

Emily burst through the water's mirror. She sat upright and gasped while her mother crossed her arms.

"There you are."

Water droplets dripped from Emily's hair and splashed into the creek below. She wrung her hair.

"How's the water?" Though Ma's lips were pursed, they seemed to twitch into a slight smile, as if she remembered the days of her youth. She wiped perspiration off her forehead with the back of her hand.

"Oh, it feels glorious."

Ma snatched the dress lying on the bank and extended it toward Emily. "Put on your dress and come back to the house."

"Aw-w-w, do I hafta?" Emily took the dress from her mother and slipped it over her wet chemise. "It's so hot in the house, even with the windows open."

"I guess we could sit outside in the oak tree's shade. Now hurry, we don't have much time before I have to start supper."

Emily stared longingly at the cool creek. She would rather be in the water than doing whatever chore Ma assigned her.

"Emily!" Ma called, stopping on the path that led to their small farm.

"Coming."

Ma waited until Emily caught up before continuing on the game trail. As they walked along the worn pathway, the birds chattered and sang songs in the trees.

Outside the creek's oasis, grass stalks remained still across an ocean of open prairie. Emily missed seeing their feathered tails sway in the breeze. A gust of wind would be welcomed. The unpredictable Midwestern weather showed them no mercy today. Emily's chemise had dried under the sun's powerful heat, and now sweat soaked through. She wrinkled her nose at the unpleasant body odor.

Beyond the tall grass, her father and three older brothers worked the fields. They each took turns breaking sod with a plow and horse. Another two years and the one hundred sixty acres would be theirs. Homesteading in Dakota Territory had come at a price.

Emily's gaze meandered past the men and stopped at the wooden fence that marked their family cemetery. An ache flooded her. Life's frailty had claimed her youngest brothers and sisters and grandparents. It wasn't fair. Why had they gotten it and not the rest of the family?

"You comin', Emily?" Ma asked.

Emily skipped to where she stood waiting.

Ma leaned forward, hands resting on her knees. Her cheeks had grown flushed, and sweat rolled down her face. She panted.

"Ma, you feelin' all right?"

"Uffda. Sure is hot today."

Upon closer examination, the bluish-purple rings under Ma's eyes seemed noticeable against her skin's pallor. "Answer me, Ma."

"I'll be fine once we're in the shade."

"You don't look fine."

"Emily, I'm just tired," Ma snapped and headed toward the house. For every step she took, Emily had to double hers.

"How 'bout you rest, and I'll go get what we need?"

Ma did not reply. She staggered to the oak tree that had been here long before their arrival. A 'miracle tree,' she called it. Emily suspected a bird or squirrel had planted it by God's hand. Trees did not grow without help.

When Ma reached the shade, she slumped against its thick trunk between two protruding roots. She used an apron to mop her face. "I need a drink of water. Please bring me my sewing basket too."

Emily darted to the log cabin Pa and her three brothers had finished building last month. After living in a soddy for three years, the house seemed luxurious with its wooden floors and a cast-iron stove. Her favorite feature was all the light that shone through the windows.

Inside, Emily grabbed Ma's sewing basket that sat beside a chair in the parlor. She took a bucket from the kitchen and hurried to the well. Emily pushed aside the cover. After setting the sewing basket on the well's ledge, she lowered the bucket and rope until she heard a splash. "Finally," she muttered, hoisting the bucket.

Her elbow bumped into the basket, and it fell forward. Emily released the rope with a gasp but snagged the basket handle. A small plop came from below. Something had fallen from Ma's sewing basket, but what? She placed the basket on the ground. Ma needed a drink of water more than the missing item. Emily returned to the shade of the oak tree with the water and sewing basket.

Ma's eyes were closed, and a light snoring came from her.

"Ma?"

"Hm?"

"I brought you water."

Ma straightened. Her finger traced the bucket's curved handle. "No dipper?"

Emily's shoulders drooped. In her haste, she had forgotten it in the kitchen.

Ma dipped her hands into the water and formed a cup shape to drink from. When she finished drinking, she splashed water on her face. "Thank you. That water feels heavenly."

"I ... something fell out of your sewing basket and into the well." Emily averted her mother's gaze.

Fabric rustled as Ma rummaged through the sewing basket. She laid out colorful material on the brown grass beside her, releasing a soft crunch with each movement. Blue, red, and yellow soon filled a small section.

Emily caressed a narrow red strip. "Are you making another quilt?"

"I thought it time that I teach you sewing, since you'll be turning thirteen. It's an important skill for a wife to have, and it'll help you find a job anywhere." Ma smiled. "That's how I met your pa."

"But Ma-a-a."

"Every afternoon, you and I will do sewing lessons. When your sewing skills get better, we'll work on a patchwork quilt for your hope chest."

"I'm never getting married," Emily muttered.

Ma laughed and ruffled Emily's hair. "You're just as much a tomboy as I was when I was your age."

"What do the three colors mean?"

"Blue, red, and yellow represent three things in a marriage and life." Ma weaved the red strip between her fingers. "Red means love and passion. It's the most important, because it binds us together in any relationship. Without it, relationships die."

"For everyone we meet?"

Ma replaced the red strip with a blue block. "Yes. Remember what the Bible says about love?"

Emily nodded.

"Blue is the sorrow and hardships one endures throughout their life." Ma lay the blue block next to a yellow block on the grass. "Life is a balance between happiness and sorrow. That's why yellow represents happiness and prosperity."

"The Lord giveth, and the Lord taketh away," Emily whispered her mother's favorite quote.

Ma collected the fabric and tucked them inside the sewing basket. "We'll have to start our sewing lessons another day. The thread is at the bottom of the well."

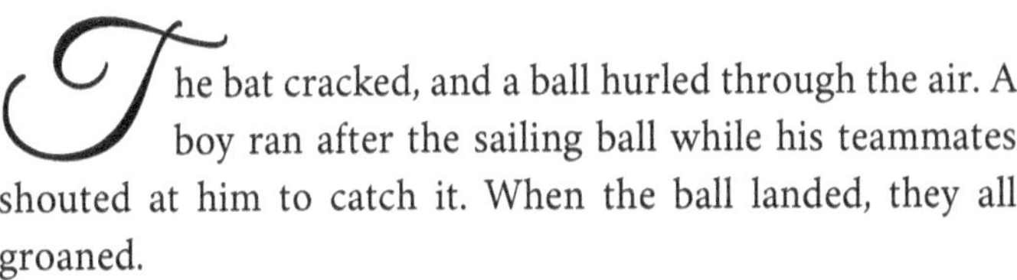

The bat cracked, and a ball hurled through the air. A boy ran after the sailing ball while his teammates shouted at him to catch it. When the ball landed, they all groaned.

Emily strolled to the ball and claimed it.

"Give the ball back," Timmy said between pants.

Emily tossed the ball and caught it. "I wanna play."

"No, you can't." Timmy reached for the ball. "You're a girl, and girls can't play baseball."

"We can too." Emily scoffed, hiding the ball behind her back.

"Cannot!"

"*Can too.*"

The tow-headed boy folded his arms. "*Cannot.*"

Emily released the ball with the flick of her wrist and threw it past him. She leaned forward until her nose touched Timmy's. "Can too."

"You're still not playing."

The third baseman waved his hand in midair and in it was the ball. He jogged the short distance. His hazel eyes held a sparkle in them as he grinned. "Hi. I'm John Knutson."

"John, tell her that girls can't play baseball," Timmy said.

"She's got a good arm on her. I think if she wants to play, we should let her."

"Are you new here?" Emily asked.

Timmy shoved John backward, causing the ball to fall. "Thems the rules. No girls allowed."

John clenched his fists at his side and glared at Timmy but said nothing. He uncurled his fists. "Find another player," John said as he walked away.

"This is your fault." Timmy grabbed the ball off the ground and shook it at her.

Emily clenched her jaw and slapped the ball free from Timmy's hand, sending the ball into a roll across the dirt. She plucked the ball off the ground. "Looks like you're short a player." She marched past Timmy's gaping mouth and smiled.

Behind her, Timmy stammered about a girl hitting him.

Emily gave the ball to a pitcher, who nodded at her. She

advanced to home plate where another boy offered a bat. The hem of Emily's dress swished as she positioned herself to hit the incoming ball. She would show those boys.

The pitcher stared at her. He tossed the ball in the air several times and caught it. Without warning, the ball screamed past her.

"Strike!" someone shouted behind her.

Emily dug the nose of the bat into the dirt before assuming her hitting position again. She had to do this, or she would prove Timmy right. Her heart sped up, and she tightened her grip on the bat as the pitcher prepared for another throw.

Everything slowed when the ball left the pitcher's hand. Emily took shallow breaths. She waited then swung her bat and connected with the ball. The ball flew upward over the pitcher.

Emily sprinted toward the first base. Three boys chased after the ball in the outfield, and Emily ran to second base. Her feet hammered the ground, not stopping once she reached second base. She swung her arms. By the time she rounded third base, it was like trying to stop a runaway horse.

The pitcher caught the ball.

Emily pumped her legs just as he threw.

John hollered, "Slide! Slide!"

Emily dropped and slid across home, followed by someone calling out safe. She rose, brushing the dirt off her Sunday best.

"*Emily Marion Larson,*" Ma said.

John jogged to Emily to give her a pat. "Way to go."

"Emily, you come with me *right now!*" Ma snapped.

"I've got to go. I'm in trouble with my ma." Emily walked to the church steps where her ma stood. She followed her into the church.

"What was that?"

"I wanted to play, but Timmy wouldn't let me. He said girls couldn't play baseball, so I showed him up."

"And you think that was right?" Ma asked, her voice softening.

"Ma-a-a. He was never gonna let me play otherwise."

"Remember what we talked about with the three colors on the quilt?"

Emily rubbed off a dirt spot on her dress she had missed. "I showed passion," she mumbled.

"Please look at me." Ma raised Emily's chin until their eyes met. Hollows had settled in where her rotund cheeks were. "You did not show love. Why d'you wanna play?"

Emily shrugged. Her gaze glided up and down at the way Ma's dress hung on her gaunt frame. She had lost more weight. What was wrong with her?

"Well?"

"I dunno." Emily shrugged again, twisting the toe of her shoe back and forth on the floor. "I get tired of being told girls can't do this, or girls can't do that. I wish I woulda been born a boy."

Ma slumped onto the bench and patted the seat beside her. "Someday you'll feel blessed to be a woman. For now, I want you to join me and the others."

An older woman with salt-and-pepper hair ambled to them. "Is everything okay, Mary?"

"Emily, this is the reverend's wife, Anna Solheim. Anna, this is my daughter Emily."

"Nice to meetcha, honey." Mrs. Solheim extended a hand toward Emily. "Are ya joining us in our sewing circle?"

Emily forced a smile as she shook Mrs. Solheim's hand.

"She is. Emily's fourteen, and I'm afraid we haven't had many sewing lessons this last year."

Mrs. Solheim glanced at the other women sewing. "We'll

help. I know you have been feeling poorly these past months."

Emily would rather go back outside than sew. She wanted to talk with John again and learn more about him. Since Emily and her family had settled here four years ago, many other people had also come to homestead in the Red River Valley, creating prairie towns overnight. Meriden was the closest they came to civilization.

"You rest," Mrs. Solheim said to Ma.

"Emily, you can work on the red border today. After you're finished, I want you to apologize to the boys for interrupting their game."

Emily scoffed.

"And while you're sewing, remember what the Bible says about love and passion."

"Yes, Ma," Emily muttered, rising from the bench.

"I forgot my sewing basket in the wagon. Could you please get it?"

Emily responded then stepped outside the church. She stood, absorbing the morning sun's heat, and found John sitting on the stairs. Guilt nibbled at her. Her selfishness of wanting to play baseball had caused John from making new friends today. Ma was right. Love and passion built relationships, even if it didn't include her.

~

Sobbing, Emily burst through the kitchen door and darted into the parlor. Ma was dead. She ransacked the sewing basket. Blue, red, and yellow fabric lay in a disheveled pile while spools rolled across the wooden floor. "I-I-I ..." Emily bawled, kicking at the quilt and loose material and careening it against the wall. She fell to her knees.

A blue block had escaped her foot. Emily picked it up and pressed it against her tear-soaked cheek.

"Blue is the sorrow and hardships one endures throughout their life," an ethereal voice said.

"I gotta finish the quilt for Ma," Emily muttered. She collected one of the runaway bobbins, unwound the thread and dropped it on the floor with a clatter. The spool rolled away farther as she fumbled with grasping it.

Her fingers trembled, making it difficult to thread the needle. Emily stuck the tip of the thread into her mouth and slid it through the needle's eye. She cut the line. "Gotta finish the quilt," she chanted quietly.

Emily held a blue and yellow square. Her vision blurred. Ma would never see the quilt finished they had started. Emily jabbed the needle in and out of the fabric until a point pricked her finger. "Ow!" she exclaimed, yanking away her finger.

Ruined. Renewed tears streaked Emily's face as she sucked on her fingertip. She had ruined the quilt with blood droplets. It was her fault for being in a hurry. Now she would have to undo the terrible seam and wash out the crimson stain.

Footsteps shuffled across the kitchen floor and into the parlor then stopped beside Emily. "Oh, honey," the reverend's wife, Mrs. Solheim, said. Arms wrapped around Emily and pulled her closer.

"I …" Emily whimpered, "ruined it."

"Shh." Mrs. Solheim stroked large circles on Emily's back. She held Emily until her tears slowed to a trickle. "Your ma's quilt isn't ruined."

"Yes, it is." Emily showed her the blood and the uneven stitches on the two blocks. "See?"

"It's still pretty. Beautiful things must have imperfections. It's a culmination of imperfections that make things seem more beautiful and make life worthwhile."

"My ma was beautiful. Why'd she hafta die?" Emily choked back a sob.

"Remember what you learned about the three colors of life?"

"That the Lord giveth, and the Lord taketh away?"

"No. For everything, there is a season." Mrs. Solheim pulled back from Emily and tucked loose stray hairs behind her ears. She examined Emily. "Although we don't understand, it was your ma's time."

"I gots no one to teach me how to sew."

Mrs. Solheim dried Emily's cheeks with a laced hankie. "You have me and the other church ladies. When you come to church, bring your sewing basket."

"Emily, are you in here?" a man asked.

"She'll be out in a jiffy, dear," Mrs. Solheim replied. She helped Emily up from the floor and straightened her dress. When Mrs. Solheim was satisfied, she nudged Emily toward the kitchen. "It's young John Knutson."

A gangly teenage boy stood fidgeting with his porkpie hat outside her door. His gaze landed on her appearance. "Emily. How are you?"

Emily shrugged.

"I wanted—" John donned his hat and stepped forward. "I'm sorry about your ma's passing."

Tears welled again. Emily took a deep breath and exhaled slowly, alleviating the tightness in her throat. "Thanks."

"Do ya wanna take a walk with me? We don't gotta talk, just walk."

"I ... I'd like that." Emily joined him outside, and together they walked side by side in silence. His presence eased a little of the loneliness within her. The Lord had giveth friends in her hour of need.

~

*E*mily set down her carpetbag in front of the dress shop. With its fresh-cut timber siding, the pristine shop stood along Main Street's collection of businesses. Meriden had boomed in two years since its conception. Each time Emily had come to town, it seemed like hammers rang out as men built businesses and houses. She missed the prairie's quietness.

Two men worked together at hanging the shop's sign, which said CHARLOTTE'S. A woman swept the newly laid boardwalk nearby. She must be the owner.

Rumors had spread around town about its newest resident, but Emily didn't care, for she needed a job. "Excuse me. Are you Charlotte?"

The woman stopped and turned. "I am. How can I help you?"

"I wondered if you might take on an apprentice."

"You're joshin' me." Charlotte leaned her broom against the post. "You've heard the rumors, I assume?"

"Yes, but that's all they are."

Charlotte's mismatched eyes bobbed as she seemed to study Emily. A smile crept across her face. "Come on in, and we'll discuss terms."

Emily followed her into the store. Inside, on one wall, fabric filled the ceiling-to-floor shelves. Ribbons, thread, and other sewing supplies were tidied in their rightful places. She gaped. Ma had worked in one of these?

"You ever been in a dress shop before?"

"No, but my ma had when she was my age."

"You must be what, sixteen or seventeen?"

"Sixteen." Emily faced the older woman and shook her hand. "I'm sorry. I've been rude in not introducing myself. Emily Larson."

"Charlotte Decane, but please call me Charlotte." Charlotte pushed aside a curtain, revealing stairs that led to the second floor. "You can bring your belongings to the guest bedroom, and then we can get started."

Emily peered through the bedroom's window at the street below busy with shoppers and horses and wagons traveling through.

A lanky man exited the general store and loaded what looked to be farming supplies. He glanced up at the window she stood at. The man seemed familiar, but the brim of his hat obscured his face.

Ma's voice whispered in her ear, *That's how I met your pa.*

A lump grew inside Emily's throat at the memory. Ma would be proud of her tomboy daughter working at a dress shop. Emily turned from the window and went downstairs where Charlotte waited on Mrs. Solheim.

"Mrs. Solheim, this is—"

"Emily!" the Reverend's wife exclaimed. She tilted forward and said in a low voice to Charlotte, "You won't be disappointed."

"How are you, Mrs. Solheim?" Emily joined Charlotte behind the counter.

"I'm doing well. Thank you for asking. My daughter and her husband are expecting their first child in the fall." Mrs. Solheim smiled, her gaze traveling toward the fabric.

Boots scraped along the boardwalk. The lanky man passed the window and appeared in the doorway.

"You want material to make a blanket for the baby, I assume?" Charlotte asked. When Mrs. Solheim replied with a yes, Charlotte walked around the counter and led her to the shelves lined with material.

"How can I help you, sir?" Emily asked the male customer.

He removed his hat. "Emily? You work here?"

"I started today." Emily squinted, examining him.

"It's me, John Knutson."

"I-I-I thought you and your family moved farther west?"

"We did, but I came back here."

John was no longer the gangly teenager who had visited her after Ma's funeral. Stubble framed John's square jaw, and lean muscles filled out his body. He had grown into a handsome man. His hazel eyes met hers, and Emily's heart fluttered.

Emily swallowed. "What brought you back?"

In the corner, Charlotte held out yellow gingham while Mrs. Solheim ran a finger across the fabric.

"Yellow stands for happiness and prosperity," Emily whispered to herself.

"You say something?"

"Oh, it was nothing. What did you need?"

"Do you ladies mend?"

"Yes, we do."

"The next time I get to town, I'll bring my mending pile." John placed the hat back on his head and paused. "Will you go to church with me on Sunday? Afterward, we could go on a picnic."

Emily nodded. "I'd like that."

"I'll come before church and walk with you."

"Sounds good. I'll see you on Sunday."

As John left, Charlotte and Mrs. Solheim chuckled. They returned to the counter with several colored fabrics, spools of thread, and needles. Charlotte began measuring.

"He moved back because he's sweet on you," Mrs. Solheim said to Emily.

Emily's cheeks grew warm.

"Looks like she's sweet on him too," Charlotte teased, cutting the material and folding it.

Emily secured the fabric bundles with twine. When Emily finished, she pointed at the yellow gingham and cleared her throat. "The yellow is an excellent choice. My ma told me it represents happiness and prosperity."

"I think you'll find happiness and prosperity with John." Mrs. Solheim clasped her hand over Emily's. "And when you do, you can put the quilt on your marital bed."

"I haven't finished it yet."

"Why not?" Charlotte asked.

Mrs. Solheim responded, "You're afraid of losing that connection with your ma, ain't you?"

Emily blinked tears close to overflowing. Mrs. Solheim was right. Ma had started this quilt three years ago, and now Emily couldn't bear to finish it. Each color she sewed held memories. She had one red rectangle and one yellow square remaining. Emily waited for a special occasion before marrying the two pieces to the quilt.

~

*E*mily's heart raced the closer she got to her new home, its pace creating a steady thump in her ears. She smoothed the fabric on her lap. A lump formed in her throat at the reminder that Ma was here in spirit. Had Ma felt this nervous as a new bride?

A warm, callused hand slipped into hers, startling Emily.

"You ready to see our home?" her husband, John, asked.

The lump in Emily's throat swelled. She settled for a nod and a tight-lipped smile.

John slowed the horses as they entered a yard containing a barn, corral, and soddy house. He stopped the buckboard and faced her. "I know it's not a proper house, but hopefully, we can build one next year if the crops and livestock do well."

"We have each other," Emily whispered.

John squeezed her hand. "Yes, we do. You ready, Mrs. Knutson?"

"Ja."

John helped Emily down from the wagon. Holding her hand, he led her to the front door of the soddy and opened it. "May I have the honor of carrying my wife over the threshold?"

His wife. She was John's wife. The word stuck on Emily's tongue like Latin, which she eventually learned. Perhaps she would learn how to be a good wife. She gave him permission and wrapped her arms around his neck as he carried her inside the soddy.

Though it was dank and dim, Emily would make the best of it for him. A longing for sunlight streaming through windows crept into her thoughts. When Emily had been a child, Ma had whitewashed their soddy walls to combat the darkness. She would do the same.

"What do you think?" John sat her on a chair at their dining table and kissed her cheek. "I'm sorry there aren't more windows. I could only afford the one."

"It'll do. We should whitewash the walls; that'll help lighten it up in here."

"The next time I go to town, I'll buy some." John moved toward the door. "I'll bring in your things, and you can make it a home."

"After I change, I can help you do chores."

"I'll do it tonight. For now, I want you to unpack and get settled before supper." John's lanky frame disappeared outside. He reappeared a minute later, toting her hope chest. "Where would you like this?"

"By the bed."

When John left again, Emily stripped the bed. She ran a hand along the soft mattress and put on the fresh sheets the ladies church circle had made for a wedding gift. Tears welled in her eyes at the colorful quilt. Emily unfolded the quilt and clutched it to her chest, slumping onto the bed.

Tears spilled onto the fabric. Ma had started the quilt but had died before finishing it. She should have been allowed the joy of being alive to watch her tomboy daughter's wedding day.

Emily pressed the quilt against her face. A roughness brushed along her skin, and she cried a little harder. It was the uneven stitches she had sewn after Ma's funeral.

Mrs. Solheim's voice whispered, *"Beautiful things must have imperfection. It's a culmination of imperfections that make things seem more beautiful and make life worthwhile."*

Emily searched near a shoddy seam and found the faint bloodstain she had left behind in her haste. She rubbed it. "I'm sorry, Ma, for fighting with you about the sewing lessons." She stifled a sob. "Mrs. Solheim and the church ladies helped me finish it." She brought the quilt closer to her chest and closed her eyes, pretending it was a hug from Ma.

"Emily?"

Emily jerked.

"Sorry, didn't mean to startle ya. You okay?"

"I was thinking about the journey this quilt has taken me through, starting when I was a girl and ending as a woman."

The mattress sank underneath John's weight. His hazel eyes flitted back and forth as he studied the quilt in Emily's arms. "You wanna talk 'bout it?"

"Help me put it on the bed?" Emily sniffled, rising. "I was thirteen when Ma decided it was time I learned to sew."

Each took a corner of the quilt, and together they draped it across the top of their feathered bed. The patchwork material displayed its splendor of colored beauty and scars. John traced a seam.

"The blue, red, and yellow each hold a special meaning in life and in a marriage."

His finger skimmed atop a blue block. "What do they mean?" he asked softly.

"Blue represents the sorrows and hardships we might endure."

"And this?" John touched the yellow square.

"Happiness and prosperity." Emily pointed at the quilt's red border. "Red represents love and passion. Ma said, 'It's the most important, because it binds us together in any relationship. Without it, relationships die.'"

John encompassed Emily with his arms and embraced her. "Your ma was a wise woman. Blue, red, and yellow are the three colors of life."

Emily inhaled his scent of earth, horse, and sweat. Ma's patchwork quilt foretold what John and she might experience in their lifetime, just like Ma and Pa had. The Lord giveth, and the Lord taketh. For now, Emily would enjoy what the Lord giveth.

FIRE

BY ALAINE GREYSON

Falcon Cortez—heir to the throne, possessor of fortunes, prince of the perfect hair—perched on his high-back leather chair at the head of the cherrywood dining table. He surveyed his posh surroundings of purple velvet drapes and deep-red carpets. The colors suited his rank and privilege but tortured his soul. Expectations had been placed upon him since birth—expectations he hadn't asked for or desired. But it didn't matter. His opinion proved useless—useless to change minds and useless to plan his own future. This was his domain, his kingdom within the small town in which he dwelled, even though he wished for something different. For decades, his family had dominated the social scene. And while not royalty, they were treated as such and afforded all the comforts and notoriety that accompanied their social distinction. His great-grandfather had started it all with his meteoric rise in the textile world sixty years ago. Each generation had added to the company that had begun manufacturing yarn and random fabrics and now expanded to include fashion design with top-tier designers and the Paris runway. *Paris.* Falcon attempted to push the memory from his mind. It only served further damage to his lonely heart. It reminded him of Cadence and the life he could never pursue. Trying to forget, he raised a wine glass to his lips and jolted at an abrupt crash, red wine spilling onto his freshly ironed white shirt.

"Should we provide bibs at meals, Falcon?" Hattie Cortez, Falcon's older sister and biggest nuisance, peered over her glass. "Or have you imbibed too much this morning? I've heard stories."

Stories. Relegating the noise to the back of his mind, Falcon twirled the glass in his hand and leaned back in his chair. "Have you, dear sister? And what stories might they be?"

"Oh, nothing much. Drunkenness, debauchery …"

A playful glint danced in Falcon's eyes. His sister teased about his active social life, but she wasn't much different. "Debauchery? That's a word I never thought would slip your lips. Is that even used nowadays?"

Hattie threw back her head and laughed. "It's appropriate. A different girl every night? Clubbing like there's no tomorrow? Are you …?"

"Am I what? On drugs?" She would be right to speculate. Falcon ran with a raucous crowd who loved fast cars and even faster women. The rich playboy scene attracted young men like Falcon who had too much money and too much time. And drugs were always plentiful. Too bad they were also tempting, since Cadence—

Falcon pushed aside the memory that had haunted his mind for far too long. It wasn't wise to dwell on something that couldn't change.

Hattie shrugged and placed a forkful of pancake in her mouth. "It's possible."

"No."

"It's not possible?"

Falcon sighed. She had missed her calling. Hattie would better serve mankind as a lawyer than an aging debutante. "I'm not on drugs." Falcon placed his glass on the table and glanced toward the door. His eyes narrowed as a loud boom and a billow of smoke filled the hallway. "What is that?"

A dark figure entered the dining room, soot covering her face. Her long black hair was piled upon her head like a bird's nest with a single pick sticking sideways.

Falcon giggled at the sight. How like his little sister, making a grand entrance to breakfast.

Madison Cortez stood a few feet from the doorway, covering her mouth while she coughed. "That wasn't supposed to happen."

Hattie rose and rushed toward the figure, alarm showing in her eyes. "Madison!" Hattie's hands brushed Madison's cheeks, wiping away the soot. "Whatever is this about? And what caused this?" Hattie stared quizzically at her blackened thumb.

"Just a small explosion. Nothing of any concern."

Falcon cleared his throat. "You interrupt my breakfast with a jolt, making me spill red wine on my freshly cleaned shirt, you enter the dining room covered in black ash of some sort with smoke billowing in the hallway and it's nothing of concern?"

Madison cocked her head. "Red wine? With breakfast?"

Falcon released an exasperated sigh. "What were you doing, Madison? And why do you insist on blowing up our house?"

"Blowing up our house, huh? It's an idea, but not my intent." Madison strolled past Hattie and reached for an apple in the center of the table. "While the two of you gallivant around town, partying and wasting your life, I'm saving the world."

Hattie placed her hands on her hips and huffed. "I don't party."

Madison crunched into the apple and chuckled. "Of course, you do. Both of you have rather colorful reputations."

"And I had planned on sticking up for you." Hattie harrumphed and returned to her seat.

"I don't need your help, thank you." Madison faced Falcon. "But you. You could use my help."

Oh great. Madison, his sixteen-year-old sister who didn't know anything about life that couldn't be found in a textbook, thought she could help him? This would be good. "And just how are you planning on helping me? I don't need any potions or explosions."

"No. But you do need some courage. What's her name again? Cadence?"

Falcon froze. How did Madison know about Cadence? She was a dalliance from his time in Paris, not a girl suitable for his position—a bothersome fact his father had drilled into his head. "Where do you get your information, little sis? Sending one of your drones to spy on me?"

A wide smile spread across Madison's face. "No, but that's not a bad idea. Perhaps I'd understand you better if I kept closer tabs."

"If you know about Cadence, you're keeping close enough."

Hattie's high-pitched voice rose above their conversation. "Who's Cadence, and why I am only hearing about her now?"

Falcon's face reddened. He couldn't let Hattie know about his Paris affair. He had promised his father he would let Cadence go, and he had kept his promise. This interference wasn't helpful. Falcon grasped Madison's elbow and pulled her into the hallway. "What's your game?"

"Game? I don't play games, Falcon."

He paced the red carpet connecting the dining room to

the front hall. "You weren't in Paris with me. You've never met Cadence, and I've never discussed her when I returned."

Madison folded her arms and leaned against the wall. "All true."

"Then what gives? Some kind of mindreading serum?"

"You think me that good?"

"I wouldn't put anything past you, dear sister."

"So formal, yet so … lost."

"Clue me in?"

"Oh, I could. But that would destroy all my fun. I think I'll let you stew a bit longer. Your eyes dance like fire when you're angry."

Falcon drew a breath. "I'm not angry, just curious. How do you know about Cadence? And what exactly do you know?"

"You really like her, don't you? She's more than a passing fancy, more than the high-society, rich bitches you've been dating."

"Watch your language."

Madison harrumphed. "Well, they're spoiled, entitled snobs. But Cadence … she's different."

Cadence was different. That's what attracted Falcon. She had no expectations, no unrealistic desires. With her, he had freedom to be himself and have fun. It was a foreign feeling, but one he relished. And one his father said he could no longer have. "I'm asking one more time. How do you know about Cadence?"

"Easy. She's here."

Falcon froze. *Here.* How was that possible? He had left Cadence in Paris six months ago. They hadn't even texted since his plane departed. Why would she be here, and why would Madison know before he did? "Stop playing games."

"It's not a game. She's here, in Meadowlark. I had lunch with her yesterday."

"And you waited until this morning to tell me?"

"I wasn't planning on telling you at all. But then I nearly blew up the house and I thought ..."

Falcon towered over his sister, his eyes menacing. "Where is she staying?"

"If I tell you, will you cover for my little ... accident?"

"Where is she staying, Madison?"

Madison dug out a business card from her pocket. "Okay, okay. Here." She thrust it in Falcon's hand. "But don't scare her away. You're quite intimidating when you're mad."

Falcon stared at the card. Cadence was here, in Meadowlark. Memories of her hair shining in the Paris sun, her inviting laugh—warm and full of life—and her adventurous spirit encouraging him to take on new experiences flashed across his mind. She was unlike anyone he had ever known, or ever would know.

"Well? Are you going or not?"

"Not your concern. Clean this mess before Father gets home. And don't think Hattie won't say something. She's not as discreet as me."

～

*S*he had made a mistake coming here. Getting involved with a Cortez was stupid enough, but to make the trip across the ocean to the small, industrial town, hoping he'd talk to her—classic idiotic move. Whatever happened in Paris was supposed to stay in Paris, right? Falcon never invited her into his life. She was a bit of fun on his vacation, a distraction from his responsibilities. What they had in Paris was pure fantasy, nothing else, so, why did she hop on a plane and invade his space? What did she hope to gain? And why did she have lunch with his sixteen-year-old sister?

Cadence sat on the lumpy bed and massaged her temples. Something wasn't right. No other man had this kind of pull —the kind that had yanked her from familiarity and comfort and had thrust her into an unknown world. She rose and reached for her suitcase. Staying here spelled disaster. If Madison had informed Falcon of her presence, he would come and drag her onto the next flight home himself. Although the thought of his hands on her, no matter how rough, ignited a fire within. Cadence threw her suitcase on the bed, startled when the door swung open.

"You're really here."

Cadence caught her breath. Her strawberry-blond hair fell around her slight shoulder, and her green eyes gazed into his smoky grays. "She told you."

"The question is, why didn't you?"

"You know the answer."

"But then why did you come?"

Cadence averted her eyes and concentrated on filling her suitcase. "I shouldn't have. I don't know what possessed me."

"I'm glad you did. I've missed you."

A tear escaped Cadence's eye. "I've missed you too. Every day, I stare at the front door of the shop, hoping you changed your mind."

"It wasn't mine to change. My father's directive—"

Cadence snorted. "Your father. He's more important?"

"I have an obligation to my family. To the business."

"To your money."

Falcon pursed his lips. "That's not fair."

"Isn't it? If you stayed with me, your father threatened to cut you off. That's why you left. It has nothing to do with obligation to family. It's all about maintaining your lifestyle and keeping your fortune."

"You weren't born into a wealthy family. You don't understand the expectations."

"Thank you for putting me in my place, Falcon. I wasn't born into wealth. But that doesn't make me less than. In fact, that makes me better, because I'm free to do what I want. And what I want to do is leave." Cadence slammed the suitcase shut.

Falcon strode toward the bed. "Cadence, I—"

"Can it. There's nothing you can say, and I was stupid for thinking something had changed. You said many things in Paris, but they don't apply to the real world."

"Are you implying I lied?"

"Not entirely. At the time, I'm sure you believed it. But I don't belong in your world, and you wouldn't be content in mine."

Falcon reached for her hands only to be pushed back. "Cadence, please."

"Go home, Falcon. Forget I exist. It shouldn't be hard, because until I showed up, you never tried to contact me."

"That's not fair. You know how I feel."

"Do I?" Cadence turned, marched toward the dresser and removed clothes she had recently placed there. "Please. Leave. I can't stand another broken heart."

Falcon wrapped his hands around her wrists and pulled her close. "I told you I wouldn't break your heart."

"And yet you did. You left me in Paris, Falcon. Alone. With no communication and no hope of a future together. And you don't think you broke my heart?" Cadence wrested herself away and turned toward the window. "I'm getting the next flight home. Goodbye, Falcon."

"Cadence."

A tear streaked her cheek. "I said, goodbye." This wasn't how she had envisioned their reunion, but could there be another way? Not without destroying what was left of her heart.

~

That hadn't gone as planned. Falcon shook his head. He had never expected to see Cadence again, so he didn't have a plan, but if he did, what had happened wouldn't have been it. He slammed on his BMW's accelerator and sped home. The farther he got from that French vixen, the better.

Falcon parked in the circular driveway and handed his keys to the waiting butler. This was his domain, where he belonged. Cadence confused things. His heritage and his responsibilities were logical and clear. He didn't need the baggage and emotional trauma his relationship with Cadence provided. He needed direction, purpose, and duty, all of which his family and the business gave.

~

"This is a house, not a laboratory. And you are a young lady, not a scientist."

"Says you. If you don't want me conducting experiments in the library, then rent a space for me downtown. I'm not stopping my experiments. I almost had a breakthrough today."

"Really? And just what are you working on?"

Madison shrugged. "I'm not sure. But when I figure it out, I'll let you know." She flashed a wide grin. "Falcon's home. Go pester him."

Victor Cortez rolled his eyes as Madison strolled toward the kitchen. "What a fine way for a young lady to talk to her father. Falcon, where did I go wrong?"

"Madison is just like you. She's stubborn, and she gets what she wants. I don't think you stood a chance from the moment she learned to talk."

"True enough. Come by my office in an hour. I want to

discuss an opportunity in Paris. I thought you might be interested."

Paris, again? That would mean he'd be in the same city as Cadence. Why was fate playing games with his emotions? Why couldn't Cadence disappear from his life and his mind? It would be easier without the constant reminder of what he couldn't have. Falcon nodded and meandered toward the kitchen. A snack would help clear his mind.

"Chickened out?"

"What? No."

"Then why are you here and not gallivanting around town, or holed up in her hotel room?" Madison crunched on an apple.

"Because. She's going home."

"Ah. You pissed her off. Good going."

"I didn't piss her off. She belongs in Paris, and I belong here."

"Except Dad has a Paris job open with your name on it."

"Did you eavesdrop?"

"When will you realize I know *everything*?"

She had a point. Madison was the fount of all knowledge in the family. "Okay, smarty pants. If you know everything, what am I supposed to do now?"

"That depends. How did you leave things with Cadence?"

"Badly."

"Not surprised. You don't understand women, do you?"

"Just tell me what I did wrong and what I need to do next."

Madison's eyes shone as a wide grin formed. "Let her go. Chasing after her now will make things worse."

"Okay. So, I do nothing."

"I didn't say that. First, you need to decide what you want. If you don't want her, make that clear. Tell her. Don't let her assume. Give her some closure."

If he didn't want her …? Falcon closed his eyes and pictured Cadence, her arms crossed and anger spread across her face. She was hurt, broken, and it had been his fault. He didn't want to cause more pain. "I'm not trying to hurt her."

"I know that. But does she?"

"This is too complicated for a teenager to understand." Falcon strode toward the refrigerator and retrieved a carton of milk.

"Do you want her, Falcon?"

"It doesn't matter what I want. Father doesn't approve."

"Because she's a seamstress and not a debutante? Aren't we passed that kind of prejudice?"

"Apparently not, according to Father."

"Ridiculous. If that wasn't an obstacle—and it's stupid one—do you want her?"

Falcon poured some milk and sloshed it inside the glass. Did he want her? That was a stupid question. Of course, he wanted her. But he couldn't defy his father. Or could he?

"Answer the question. It's not hard. You have the opportunity to live and work in Paris, with Cadence. And Dad won't be anywhere in sight, except for the occasional visit. If you don't jump on this, you're more of an idiot than I thought."

Was he an idiot? At this point, Falcon didn't know what to think … or feel. This morning Cadence had been a memory of forgotten love. And now … what was she now? What could she truly be? And more importantly, what did he want her to be?

~

*P*iles of fabric filled every nook of the small shop. Cadence's few employees had tried to keep up with orders, but without Cadence's direction, it became a futile task—much like her trip to the states. She regretted her trek to Meadowlark. Not only was it expensive and a waste of time, seeing Falcon had opened the wound she had carried the past six months.

The only way through before had been work. The only way through now had to be the same. The backload of orders helped because she wouldn't spend time dreaming of Falcon. Seeing him in that bed and breakfast room resurfaced feelings of longing. When he had touched her, she wanted to give in and devour him on that lumpy bed. But she had pushed him away. She hadn't allowed him to explain, which defeated her purpose of going. The pain had become too great and seeing him increased it. If he had stood there and reminded her of why they couldn't be together, she might never have recovered. No. It was safer to go away and never look back.

"A gentleman at the door says it's urgent he speak to you."

"Tell him to come back this afternoon. I have a hard deadline with the costumes for the opera."

"He's insistent. He said he won't go away until he talks to you, even if he has to wait all day."

Cadence rolled her eyes. "Yvette, please take over. And mind the stitches. We don't need them to pop when Madame Duveny hits the high notes." Cadence smoothed her shirt and marched toward the front of the shop. She hoped this wasn't another unsatisfied customer that had waited beyond a deadline. As she approached, a familiar voice filled the air.

"I understand she is busy, but I must see her. It's urgent."

Him. Had he followed her from Meadowlark? And why?

"Please understand, sir. We are behind on orders, and Mademoiselle is quite busy. You can leave your contact information—"

"That's not good enough. I said I can wait. She must take a break at some point."

"But, sir, we're a small shop, and you are taking up important space."

"Diane, that's enough. Go help Yvette with the opera costumes." Cadence eyed her visitor and leaned against the reception desk. "Disturbing my workplace? Haven't you caused enough havoc in my life?"

"Cadence. You look amazing."

"I look tired. I've been working sixteen-hour days, trying to catch up from my foolish trip to Meadowlark. Biggest mistake of my life."

"You didn't let me get a word in. If you would have let me explain—"

"Explain what? We had a magical time, and I fancied myself in love. But then your father determined I wasn't good enough for you, and instead of fighting for me, you left without a word. You're a coward. Get out of my shop."

"No. You're right. I didn't fight for you, and I should have. Maybe that was cowardly. But I'm here now."

"And for that I should thank you? I cried every night for six months, wondering what I did wrong and how I could fix it. But I can't fix you. Go home and tell Madison it's too little too late."

"Madison did encourage me to come."

"I know. She's wily, that sister of yours. She convinced me to fly to Meadowlark. She thought if you saw me again, you couldn't resist. She was wrong."

"Madison contacted you? How did she even know you existed? She isn't very forthcoming."

"Apparently she read your journal. Should I be flattered that at least you write about me?"

"My journal. That explains it. And yes, I do write about you. Almost every day."

"That's sweet, I suppose. But it doesn't change anything.

Go home to your privileged life, Falcon. Stop messing up mine."

"I can't. Father has put me in charge of the Paris office."

Falcon. Working in Paris? Great. "And you accepted? Idiot."

"Will you stop calling me an idiot? That reflects badly on you, since you're in love with me."

Cadence chuckled. "In love with you? A bit arrogant, don't you think?"

"You cried every night after I left. You flew to Meadowlark to see me again. And you sent your employees away to talk to me even though you're behind schedule. You're in love with me."

He was right. She was in love with him. But he didn't need confirmation of that fact. "Of all the boneheaded, self-centered things to say. Get out of my shop, Mr. Cortez."

"Your eyes are like fire when you're angry." Falcon grinned. "I'm fighting for you this time, Cadence. And I'm not giving up."

Her eyes misted as Falcon waltzed out the shop door. He was in Paris and he wanted to fight for her. That knowledge alone lit a fire inside—a fire only Falcon could ignite. And one only he could extinguish. Cadence drew a breath and marched toward the back of the shop. Finally, he was the Falcon of her dreams.

THE GREY

BY LO POTTER

I had to accept that, for my life to move on, I needed to leave that place. Having been mourning for seven years, I'd been standing still, holding onto a part of me I felt I never owned—instead, praying for ghosts. I signed a three-month contract to relieve myself of what my brother wrote to assure me was a "widower's lament." His words waxed of our father's time on whaling ships when my brother was a young boy sent away after the death of his mother, long before I was born. Until now, I'd worked in acetylene beacon management at the outposts along the shores of the sound, enjoying the comforts of proximity to Fort Lawton and wasting away in my own stagnation, pickling in the stench of the briny rye of my surrounding peers. Many had gifted me bottles that sat corked, though I brought them along to this new assigned post at their behest. Reading my brother's words and speaking to my superiors, I found the assignment appealing. They reminded me electrification would soon relieve me of my position ashore, and the outer lighthouses without generators were where I ought to be moving on. But I had not realized spring would be naught but grey fog. A "June Gloom" they called it, starting in April of every year.

As our small steamer's foghorn spilled over the rolling wafts of mist, I stared at the approaching lighthouse silhouette on the westernmost edge of the Puget Sound. Beyond it lay the vacant ocean, vanishing in the blended gradient of clouds and fog reflecting off the water, as if I were suspended somewhere else in time and space—another world entirely.

The boatman left my sack ashore with the crates of supplies and replacement calcium carbide as he loaded the dazed former keeper. That quiet man with dark circles under his eyes glanced at me only once, shook his head then crawled onto the boat and slumped into his seat with a thud. He snored as the boatman pulled from the crag with the assurance he would return on the first of each month to provide a new supply of cans and jars.

Toward the evening, the clouds parted enough to reveal the sun staining the grey, tinged with rosy hues. Basking, the corners of my mouth twitched against my beard in a way I had all but forgotten as that tangerine sun nestled itself beneath the waves. I wrapped myself in the salt-encrusted blanket and ascended the tower's spiral metal staircase. There the acetylene torch burned, and I was to maintain my strict instructions to never allow it to extinguish. Out on the walk, I listened to the distant lapping of waves through nothingness. Staring at the western horizon, I prayed her dead hands would finally release me. Perhaps this grey place would bring me peace.

In the morning I awoke to grey. It seeped through the walls. Its sticky fingers pried apart my eyelids and clung to my skin as I stared through the warped glass of the small studio's windows. In thick strokes of sea waves, it blended with the sounds of unseen birds and a haunting call I had not heard before. It murmured in the distance, yet I felt it in my bones. I shook my head to dispel it as a figment of my imagination. No creature of Heaven nor Earth could make such an unearthly call. Perhaps this outpost of solitude played tricks on the mind in this mist that swallows ships upon the sea.

Acetylene lights burn with an indescribable heat. While in the tower, I recalled my instructions. I descended the ladder then checked the depth and adjusted the flow rate by turning the gas release valve at the top of the ladder depending on the shape of the flame, just like I had been shown in my years of experience onshore. *Adjust the amount of light relative to the new moon, look for the size of the fishtail flame.* I rationed the calcium carbide and maintained a safe rate of gas production by adjusting the water flow.

I spent most of my time ascending and descending the helical stairs to reach valves at the top and bottom of the lighthouse tower. As I spent my hours listening to the hisses of the internal equipment, I had yet to see the shadows or hear the horns of a passing vessel upon the ocean waves just beyond the confines of these walls.

I descended the ladder for the final fuel check before I slept when, in the distance, a low sighing cry whimpered beneath my feet. With enough calcium carbide to shine limelight through the night until morning, I crawled up the spiral stairs into the blinding lighthouse and onto the walk where a fine mist soaked through my clothes. There, I heard my Julianna's murmur for the first time in seven years.

I collapsed to my knees and dragged myself back into the light and through the trap to descend the stairs. My heart raced as her lullaby echoed behind me, following me down as I grasped the railing to maintain my footing. Returning to the small, attached hut, I shoved my lantern upon the dressing table and stared at my face in the mirror.

No being of Heaven nor Earth ...

The low song faded into the distance as I turned to the moonless darkness outside the twisted glass. My Julianna and our child were no more; these torments of the mind were simply that and nothing more.

Through restless dreams, I heard her songs, and within weeks, I no longer slept at night. *My Julianna ...* I walked upon the crag to meet her when I heard her vibrating hum rise from beneath my feet. A splashing torrent in the distance moaned her song across the sea spray. I remembered my father's stories around the hearth of mysterious beings beneath the sea. *Could it be? My beautiful fawn-haired love cast out to forever be a spirit among the waves?*

I returned to my quarters and retreated beneath damp woolen blankets until my mind insisted I resume my duties beneath the enigmatic shifting mists.

I would track each time I checked the fuel levels and topped off the calcium carbide or adjusted the flow rates of water or gas to change the flame. I did this judging by the sun or phase of the moon, but lately, having reviewed my notes, I noticed discrepancies in my work. The cistern remained unmeasured, as I found it consistently full, perhaps by condensation of the thick mists and the frequent rain passing overhead.

Perhaps my contract's initiation on April first came from a tradition unbeknownst to me—lighthouse keeper's humor? Having arrived to keep the lamp lit at all hours to ensure the safety of all souls who passed—lost or otherwise—I spent my days checking water-stained task lists to prevent idle moments from stealing my thoughts. These sorts of jobs, consigned by contract, only sought those souls lost enough to find this place of their own free will—a place of isolation, canned bread, chamber pots, and tinged cistern water always tasting of rust.

Each day, I awake to a grey sky over grey seas. I have yet to see the sun. I question its existence. I wrote in my journal, reminding myself of the limited time a three-month contract commits.

Looking over the hurricane glass next to my drained ink pen, her voice penetrated the floorboards. "Joachim …"

For the first time in seven years, I followed my shaking hands to the cupboard where I'd stowed the gifts from my peers I'd sworn I'd never open. I pulled the cork from one of the bottles of rye.

"Julianna …" I murmured to the walls of my solitary prison, fixated on the open bottle. I gritted my teeth. The first drink burned my throat and nostrils as it flowed into the black hole inside me. Grimacing, I rattled the bottle against the tabletop as I set it down, searching the dark world outside the glass window of my hold on this rock for the source of her voice. The half-moon traversed a veiled sky above while the waves crashed against the crag below, yet I could not find a whisper of that voice.

I stared in the shaving mirror, meeting my gray eyes she once captured with hers of icy blue. *Surely the isolation and occult weather must be responsible for these phantoms.* I thought of the keeper before me, his wizened expression and distant eyes. Perhaps this was my punishment for being unable to recover my life after the loss of her and our son's lives in a single night those seven years ago.

Returning to the rye, I paced my quarters and took another drink. *No. Not by my employer's fault—they didn't mislead me.* Nor by my fault—I had chosen this for the purpose of solitude to depart from the imprisonment I experienced each day in my normal life along the shore. This small rocky outcrop jutting from the ocean lent nothing for any fog to burn off with the aid of the sun. I failed to see the land, nor was I certain how far away it even was in a reality beyond books and maps. These maritime relics stated my post stood twenty nautical miles from the nearest land—from any civilization. *An idle mind plays tricks, that's it.*

I dreamt of her sweet coldness. Her long delicate fingers caressed my face as she whispered in my ear her prophetic dreams, how she prayed for a man with eyes like winter skies, a love intense like a flame to gunpowder—the dream swirled into cannon blare.

I recalled her jubilance in all manner of speech. How I missed our conversations and her enchanting wit, her ability to bring forth my laughter unmatched by my salacious friends. I reached out to her, the insatiable need to hold her possessing me one more time. I neared, my hands so close my fingertips reminded me of the sensation of her silken hair. But her eyes rolled back as her head tipped, and a buzzing black maw opened, emitting the sound of a foghorn blasting upon the sea.

I fell from the cot as the lighthouse blew its foghorn a second time—a predictable measure of built-up gas in the tower being released in pairs every few hours. I scrambled to the lighthouse's walk to survey the conditions and adjust the flame.

Our silent doppler beacon drained the landscape of color beneath the full moon. The beam ran its blinding light through the mists, bleaching the world in its path.

I paused. *The full moon?* With the new moon and the waning gibbous so close in time, I rubbed my eyes. *Was that yesterday, the day before, or a month ago? When did the supply ships arrive? What about the logbooks?*

I rushed down the stairs to check the logbooks and the calcium carbide tank level. The ledger revealed regular checks of thirty-nine cycles of night and day since my arrival. But … when I was left here, I was told a supply ship would deliver more canned food on the first of each month, but it had not yet come. May first could not have passed yet, because the shipment hadn't arrived. Something was amiss. Some of my days were longer than others, while others were shorter. The mysterious songs were twisting my sense of time and space.

I believe she is out there in the waves. She's come to see me again. Perhaps he was the boatman of the river Styx, and I am dead, here to join her. Is death an illusion? Or is that time? Is this how my Julianna has returned to me? Time must be the illusion, for I have yet to see the supply ship.

The May first ship arrived. I ran to greet the only man aboard the vessel. "Captain, did you have safe travels? Were you at all delayed?"

He raised an eyebrow and chewed the pipe clenched between his teeth. "No." He handed me a crate with a grunt.

I placed it upon the shore. "So today is the first of May?" My own voice sounded foreign as the waves crashed behind us.

"Aye." He handed me a second crate with a considerable grunt, rolling his eyes. "Ye been keepin' yer watch wound?"

He unloaded more calcium carbide, and I cast my gaze at my feet, taking the chain he handed me. We hoisted the load onto the shore, exchanging it for the slaked lime waste. I secured the new calcium carbide supply to the hand truck, the other supply crates stacked to its side, and he pushed off with barely a farewell. "I'll see ye in thirty days."

I nodded. The coal-powered engine sputtered to life as the steam pressure built; the boatman pulled gear levers once he was in deep enough water. Within moments, I could no longer see his yellow slickers, and once again, my only companions on this rock were the lighthouse, this grey fog, and whatever it hid from my senses.

I heaved the drum of calcium carbide along the path to the lighthouse and chained it in the dry storage room. After closing the door, I checked the level of the current block through the small window and jotted the time and level into the book before returning for the remaining crates of supplies. Returning up the path with the crates loaded on a two-wheeled handcart, I approached the peeling clapboard as the icy winds blustered from the west. As I looked across the water, the faintest impression of whitecaps emerged amongst the desolate fog as the astringent smell of a hard freeze set into my senses. I had been warned a sudden cold snap could come down from Alaska, so I hurried inside and closed the stormers with their sturdy latches as I prepared to climb the stairs to the light.

"Joachim …" her whisper echoed through the hold as I strode toward the staircase.

I shook my head; a storm brewed on the horizon, and I must adjust the light.

As the mix of ice and rain pelted the rocky outcrop, the Fresnel lens sent a glow into air as thick as smoke. While the icy assault on my shelter taunted me through the structure's metal roof and shaking walls, I reassured myself that the lighthouse had survived worse storms. The acetylene burned as bright as the storm allowed, and I attempted to sleep in the howling darkness below.

"Joachim …" Julianna beckoned me as I drifted to sleep, the bottle of rye on the nightstand.

Sometime in the night, she stood in the room as the waves thundered against the crag.

I stared, uncertain how to react to my wife in her wedding gown, same as the day I married her, yet also the same as she wore the day I buried her only a few years after. "Julianna," I whispered as she lifted her eyelids and met my petrified gaze.

She knelt at my bedside and took my hand between her own. They felt as cold as the icy waters surrounding the shores. "Joachim …" The corners of her mouth spread into a devilish grin. "I knew you'd come for me. You always want to make me happy, don't you?"

My breath caught in my lungs; my panic increased, unable to inhale or exhale.

"Shh, shh … it only takes a moment. And then we'll be together forever, just like I always wanted. I always dreamed of a man with warm gray eyes like clouds over a stormy sea." Her hand moved to my chest and held me down as I struggled in my attempts to breathe.

I awoke, coughing water from my lungs, the droplets from the ceiling flowing over my face and into my mouth. The storm outside raged on as I pulled the bedframe to the side and away from the stream of water. The building shuddered as a creaking wail churned against the rocks outside. Rushing to the calcium carbide tank, I rested a hand on my chest, felt the rise and fall of my breath and nodded as I confirmed the level was as expected. As I felt my way along the staircase to the light, a splitting, scraping sound in the distance caught my attention.

The heat from the lamp fogged the glass against the outside world beyond recognition, and I failed to decipher the noise beyond a vibrant red glow. With the moaning growl of some destruction of a grinding, twisting hull upon these jagged rocks evident, I rushed back down to search for my slickers, ignoring her calls.

"Joachim …"

Now that I was fully armored in slick rubber, the wind whipped around me and pushed me about the walkway as I attempted to find the source of the devastating sounds.

"Joachim …"

*P*elted by hail, I stared across the water, shielding my eyes from the tempest's wrath. Through the maelstrom, I heard her behind me in the torrential wind whipping around me. I recalled Julianna's desire to destroy things when I would fail her, the bruises from these elements setting into my arms through my coat. I spied a distant burst of orange emerging and emanating through the darkness—a cargo steamer astray from the deep channel leading in toward American waters.

"You did this." Her final words in life had accused me, now relayed by this phantom again.

How many souls aboard? Did they even see this light? Hear the foghorn? I stared in silence as the red glow sank into darkness. As I opened the door to return, a cold hand gently rested upon my neck. I hurried but fell over the threshold and clamored to regain my stance as I braced and latched the door.

As the storm cleared, no trace of the sound's source nor light remained, though now she kept me constant company as I worked to maintain and repair my post. From the corner of my eye, she stood there, her arms crossed, as if it were ten years prior while I built our homestead along the shore. I shook the image from my mind and felt the stripped, weathered clapboard siding with my hand.

"Our child's room needs plenty of lights. He'll be your son. We'll give him a legacy, and I'll let nothing stand in his way." She held her hands to the wall in my periphery as I repainted the walls on this rare clear day with broad strokes. Her belly expanded beneath her dress. "And he'll have my father's name. He'll be a great man in this world. We can only hope he's a more successful man than you. We always hope that of the next generation, don't we?"

Her tone sounded saccharine and optimistic, so I turned

to remind her our son had never come to be. Instead, a gathering of seagulls hopped amongst debris washed upon the shore. "Damn birds," I muttered, throwing the paintbrush. The seagulls hopped away from the splattering paint but otherwise ignored my outburst.

In the coming days, I took to walking along the rocky embankment at low tide, straining my eyes for signs of life among the flotsam at my feet and confirming my fears of the previous stormy night as the remains of a ship gathered at the shore. While some creatures scurried about in the solemn waves, the sands shifted beside me. The tide turned, the water rising.

"Joachim, why do we do this? You're the youngest son, and I love you more than anyone else. Look at your own family—not a penny left to show for your devotion to your father. They left you these strange belongings; even your mother abandoned you after your father never returned from his last trip to sea." Julianna blocked my path, wearing the blue dress from the night I had proposed. "We could head west, leave this place and start a new life. Abandon the same people who've forsaken you."

I remembered how her icy-blue eyes sparkled that day, but as I returned my gaze from my thoughts to the eyes of this apparition, she vanished. The pages of my journal reflected these memories. *Once a shadow in my periphery, she grows bolder with each day.*

Soon, she remained my constant companion as I went about my tasks. She critiqued each aspect of my work with disapproving glances.

By the June delivery, she constantly chattered in my waking hours—I assumed her an apparition of madness. "Shut up," I commanded; the supply boat moored.

"That's no way to speak to your wife! You've never

spoken to me in such a disrespectful tone before." Her eyes darkened as she faded into the open cabin door.

~

We heaved the dry barrels and supply crates with grunts and exchanged silent nods and glances.

"Next time I'll bring your replacement, and you'll need to be ready," he stated without acknowledging my existence. "Reconcile the books before we arrive," he gruffed. "And eat more. You're looking thin."

I nodded, recognizing my unkempt state, as he hoisted the rope and shoved off again.

"One more month and you'll be headed to shore."

I turned toward my keep and saw her staring at me through the window, a smirk creeping across her face. I checked the logbooks and dates in an attempt to reconcile the calcium carbide use and time as my reprieve from the fog faded into this suspension from civilization. By the sixth full moon in my three-month stay, I became suspicious. My only way to tell time was the cycles of light and dark—the impenetrable darkness broken only by a double vision as I stared at what could be either sun or moon. I had never before missed the tapping of a telegraph operator. "Perhaps electrification won't be a curse," I grumbled.

Julianna cackled in choppy bird song as she watched me struggle over the books. "So, this is what you've been doing? Some lighthouse keeper you are. You're not much better than the boy I met, still struggling to do anything on his own."

I slammed my stopped watch as it refused to be wound, the spring broken inside. "Woman, what is it you want? Our promised child took you from me. I came here to start new. Instead, you curse my time and taunt me."

Her mouth twisted into sick, pursed lips. "You did this to yourself." Her eyes clouded over like those of fish at the markets of small towns along the sound, and her mouth fell open at an unnatural angle. Her head tilted as the strange unearthly song filled the air, her mouth unmoving. She stood in the kitchen of our homestead, smashing the only plates we owned—relics of an old world.

I dropped to my knees, begging her forgiveness in tears.

Her ice-blue eyes lowered to meet my own as her mouth twisted into a satisfied smile. Her smile faded as she vanished.

The crashing of broken glass somewhere in the studio jerked me from my slumber in the chair at my desk.

"Joachim …" she whispered, a wind whistling through the gaps in the walls.

The sky darkened as I ran in search of the source. Next to the bed, the empty bottle of rye lay broken on the floor. My matted hair clung to my head beneath my cap as I grabbed the straw broom and tin dustpan. As I crouched, the darkness fell, and I had yet to light the lamp. A cold sweat dotted my forehead as her face stared at me through the window, a handprint forming across the glass.

"Joachim …" she moaned as I felt through the darkness to dispose of the broken bottle pieces in a wastebin. "Hold me. I'm in the water. Come to me."

A great fire burned within my chest. I growled, hurled myself from the room toward the carbide tank to adjust the flame and climbed the stairs to that great Fresnel lens as the lantern spun from the heat. As I ascended into that hellish tower, her devil's voice persisted.

"Joachim … Jump to the rocks and meet me in the sea."

No beast of Heaven nor Earth …

"Julianna, leave me," I whispered, my head in my hands as I curled into a ball between the window and the light.

Outside, the grey threatened to consume me, unable to tell in what existence of time and space I floated as I listened for my Julianna once more.

I must have slept in that room, for I awoke to a darkness, the calcium carbide reactions having expended themselves through the storm.

"Joachim …" she sang through the mists. "Come to me …"

I stepped onto the walk, my eyes adjusting to the night. The heavens illuminated with stars in a dazzling glow I had never witnessed as I looked to Polaris. In a moment of clarity, the fog having dissipated, the heavens touched the sea and blended into a singular expanse.

"Joachim …" In the distance, something moved beneath the waves. Great spouts of water shot into the air. "Meet our child … Do not leave me …"

I recalled being a small boy on my father's knee, holding his scrimshaw knife in my small hands. I'd traced my small fingers along the scene he'd carved into the whale ivory some ancient time ago—the great clouds over beasts surrounded by ships at sea.

A pit opened inside me, the realization I had let the light extinguish and endangered the vulnerable souls I promised safe passage. Scurrying down the steps, I felt through the darkness for my lamp and striker then hurried to the tank room. I turned the release valve to the minimum and felt my way through the darkness. I proceeded to refill the tank with calcium carbide blocks and ignored her monstrous calls as they drifted out to sea.

"Joachim …"

No beast of Heaven nor Earth … but perhaps a beast of the sea …

On my hands and knees, the striker in my teeth, and the lamp in one hand, I clamored up the steps, the metal slick with condensation. I applied the striker to the hiss of acetylene to reignite the flame then returned down the steps to adjust the intensity. Having restored the limelight, I retreated to the small bed and extinguished my lantern. There, I sat waiting to hear the return of Julianna's song.

In this abysmal darkness, I relived the night of her death when we had returned to our home in a joyous delirium to greet our promised baby boy. With rye on my breath, the midwife's funereal gaze had opened the door, her lips forming words I had failed to comprehend—*breach birth* and *hemorrhaging*. My Julianna lay dying, holding the remains of our child in a blood-soaked bundle, our bed, too, soaked in the torrent of her blood.

"Joachim …" she had spoken when she tried to reach for me. "You did this …" Her last words had fallen from her with a final breath.

As tears streaked my face, I drank the rye. In this darkness, I sobbed alone. "No," I whispered to the shadows. "I did nothing."

In my dreams, she came, her face ashen as the day I had buried her. "Joachim …" Her cloudy eyes were unmoving, her mouth falling to one side. She proffered the bloody bundle containing the corpse of our son, his body misshapen and twisted by the person I now recognized Julianna truly to be. "Hold him. Join me. Join your family."

I placed my hands on her shoulders and shook my head. "No, Julianna." I turned away. "You are not my only family."

Each night, she visited with the same request, and each day, she faded farther into the shadows as I focused on my work and climbed to the walk to watch the strange creatures singing beneath the sea. Their waterspouts and tails breached the surface in family groups as they passed the crag, heading north.

On July first, I climbed aboard the supply ship and slumped into the soft weathered teak. The new keeper waved and smiled as he passed, his fresh, young face and cheery words lost to the beckoning, lapping waves against the hull. Glancing upward toward the lighthouse's walk, I saw her ashen face glare as she rocked the rotting blood-soaked bundle I'd never meet. I closed my eyes, and the boat jerked as it shoved off into the choppy seas. Peering back, I saw her visage fade into the mists, and the sun burst through the clouds for the first time in three months as we neared the larger islands of the coast, the lighthouse lost to the distant horizon.

A DARKER SHADE OF PINK

BY JINNY ALEXANDER

*R*ose had never liked pink—a washed out younger sibling to red, a hand me down, faded color of 'Is she just as sweet as her sister?' and 'Do you think they'll be alike?' A color without vibrancy, nothing original about it.

She'd show them.

Rose waited, quietly, secretly, the paleness of her smudging at the edges of the greys in the dusty nook between the pantry door and scullery. She matched her breath to the creep of the spider.

In scuttle to the center of the web.

Out scurry to the thread that led away into the black shadow where the old wooden door didn't quite meet its frame.

In peeping out, tentative legs testing tremulous silk.

Out back to the center—the eye of web.

She wondered what the spider thought of her—a tall, thin girl, hair in untidy braids, pink. Always pink. Perhaps the spider didn't think she was tall. She was though; she only had to glance across to the other side of the doorframe to see the irregular strokes of pencil gouged into the wood. There was at least an inch between the last two marked in untidy scrawl with her name: *Rose*. She was growing quicker than Ruby now. Maybe she'd catch her soon.

Then she could be red, too. Careful not to disturb the spider, or reveal her hiding place, Rose stretched slowly, silently, onto her tiptoes, tightening her tummy until it pushed her back straight, pulling up her neck until it was as tall as the tallest pine trees in the forest. She tried to assess how many more inches she needed, but, as she strained to see the *Ruby* scratches, she wobbled, outstretched her hand to balance herself, and quickly lowered her body again onto the stability of her whole feet pressed firmly against flagstones.

It wasn't time yet.

Ages passed.

Listening, waiting, listening, waiting.

A mouse, silent as a girl in faded pink, twitched its tail as it peered at Rose from behind an old, empty wooden crate. Ancient stenciled letters may have told its name: **M O** something **S**.

Mama would say it never read MOUSE even when the writing was whole and new, but Rose couldn't tell how Mama could be certain of that.

Mouse—Mos, she'd call it, then she'd have to be right— moved closer. Slowly, slowly, a nibble forward, a jerk back, then nearer again, braver with each step as Rose stayed frozen like the ice in a pitcher of summer lemonade.

She was a bit thirsty, come to think of lemonade. *Not yet.*

The mouse, brave as a pirate, touched its whiskery nose to the toe of Rose's boot, and Rose lifted her toe in silent warning. The mouse, disappointed to have been tricked by a not statue who was a real girl, albeit a pink one, ran behind the crate, under the gap in the floor, and away to a different adventure.

Rose wished she could duck under the floorboards after it, be a big girl in a small kingdom, the leader of the mice, who would bring her a golden crown on a scarlet cushion and—

Beyond the larder door, a stripe of orange spread across the floor, widening into a wedge of golden cheese, before narrowing again with a creak and a click as the front door opened, let in the sun, and closed again to hold out the day. Rose let her shoulders flop, made her breath come out in a rush, and wriggled one foot to make it feel like it was a proper part of her and not just a playground for a mouse. It was nearly time.

She didn't need to climb onto the parlor's window ledge and press her nose onto the cold glass to know Ruby would be skipping down the path, basket hooked into the crook of her arm, boots neatly laced with scarlet ribbons, and her red cloak hugging around her as if it was made to fit—not like Rose's, Rose's faded pink cloak would flap around her as if it was a skin she'd never grow into. Ruby would be reaching out to unfasten the gate, flip up the latch, and shimmy through the gate like a dance, not a single part of her brushing against the rust or the damp mossy patches that clung to the twisty iron gate. Rose had watched Ruby walk this path so often she only had to close her eyes and lean against the scullery wall, and she could imagine it better than if she saw it. She had tried to teach her ears to hear the gate latch drop, but Ruby was too careful, too calm, or maybe even too far away, and Rose's ears just had to pretend it. Rose knew that if she counted slowly to thirty-four, the gate would close behind her sister, and she could move. Sometimes she liked to count elephants, other times hippopotamuses, or other animals with names long enough to trip her tongue and stretch the numbers into time. Today, she counted Mos Mouse in between each number, using her new friend as her anchor for measuring proper seconds, not fast ones that didn't work properly. One Mos Mouse, two Mos Mouse … and when she had thirty-four Mos Mouses running around in her mind, piling, climbing, scampering, twitching, then, only then, did she step from the shadows.

Rose climbed on the stool under the coat hooks and yanked at her pink cloak until it fell around her feet in a pool of patched-up cotton. She scooped it up, untangled, straightened, pulled around her shoulders, but didn't tie it. Stretching, reaching, she unlatched the door, shoved it shut with the toe of the boot Mos had sniffed at, and tripped along the garden path in her sister's footsteps, bootlaces flicking muddy specks around her ankles.

~

Rose knew the path—of course, she did—but it looked different when it was just her on her own. The trees were massive, crowding over her, helping her hide. She listened to them whisper to each other as she ducked from one thick trunk to the next, "Rose, Rose, Rose, shh, shh, …" They were her friends, her 'complices, her shelter, and she trusted them to hide her from her sister, protect her from the chance of Ruby looking behind her, turning quickly if she heard the noise of a younger, pinker sister sneaking after her. A twig cracked, as if it had heard Rose thinking of the possibility, and Rose glared angrily at her feet. "Shh!" she hissed at the broken stick, "Shh …" The trees giggled above her, and she smiled up at them, glad of their support.

The path wove through the trees in a well-worn scar, carved into the earth by Ruby's feet, Mama's feet, even Rose's, but hers were smaller, left fewer clues on the forest floor. Even now, Rose was careful not to add any more grooves to the path, and instead, she stayed behind the trees, parallel, always with the path in sight, but never letting her feet touch the dirt track. She jumped from mossy patch to yellow sunlight, from velvet green shade to the knobby grey-brown of fallen trees, a balance beam here, steppingstones there. Far away, or close by, her papa would be working, swinging his axe, choosing another of Rose's tree-friends to chop into a new table, a dresser, a milking stool for the dairy. Rose sometimes slunk into his workshop, and breathed the dying scent of sawdust, the tears of the trees piling around her feet like the sands of time. She used to feel sad for these chopped into things trees, when she was smaller, but Papa had showed her how to scoop up the sawdust, lay it carefully around the nursery forest, and watch, watch, watch, for the new baby trees to crawl from the sawdust, strong and green, peering out like periscopes to see if it was safe to grow yet. Rose liked the nursery forest. Some of the trees were as big as her and had names only Rose knew. She'd take her tea set, her teddy bear, old Soft Dog, a book, or some crayons and spread her tatty pink cape across the ground like a carpet, a raft, a bridge, or another dream, and talk to the trees that were her height. "More tea, Mrs Green?" "Shall we read today, Miss Oak?" One time, she tried to play ring a roses with her friends, but they usually preferred not moving things, like coloring or telling stories or letting the sun peep through their branches to join Rose for a picnic.

Today, Papa had left early, when Rose was s'posed to be still deep under her quilt but had really been telling Teddy it was time to not wake up and he should wait a bit longer before needing a biscuit. Of course, Teddy couldn't wait, and Rose had to take him to the kitchen. They had climbed onto Papa's lap, nestling into his beard to inhale the woody smell of him before he gently lifted her to the floor, brushed crumbs from his red and black checkered shirt, dropped a kiss on her bedhead hair and ushered her back to her room for a few more hours of sleep before her day needed to begin. From her room under the eaves, she could hear the click of the door closing below her and the crunch of heavy giant-sized boots on the garden path. Rose had counted to twenty-two red squirrels before she knew Papa would close the gate and disappear into the forest, axe over shoulder and lunch bouncing along in his knapsack.

~

A tiny brown bird hopped from the bracken, and Rose jumped, startled by its sudden interruption of her reverie. She hushed it, and it regarded her momentarily with an eye as beady as Mama's sewing box and flew away in a huff. When it fixed itself to a branch far enough away, it tweeted at her, reprimanding, as if she were too small and pink to be out alone in the forest.

Rose noticed its redbreast and stuck out her tongue, although usually the birds were her friends too. This robin was not her friend today. It had nearly tried to make her feel scared and small and too pink for being her on her own. She stuck out her tongue again and skipped away from the robin, checking her bearings. The path was still there, just where she had left it—a little to the side, just beyond the trees. She poked her head around a spindly beech, looking to see if she was too nearly catching up with Ruby. A flash of red, a swing of a cloak, far ahead, not too close, not too far. Rose was good at this. She'd show them she was big enough.

She'd heard them whispering when they thought she was sleeping—Mama and Ruby, late at night when the bedroom under the eaves was wrapped in dark and the corners of the room were the darkest bluey-purples, thundercloud greys, or black as the raven who came for Rose's toast crumbs every morning. It wasn't really fair that Rose had to go bed before

Ruby; she was nearly as big now. The scrapes of pencil on the scullery door said so, didn't they? She tried her best to stay awake, waiting for those secret moments where Mama talked to Ruby in the softest voice, quiet as a leaf falling in autumn, to not wake Rose. Rose, most nights, was not asleep. She was getting better at not being asleep, better at practicing staying awake so she could say, "I'm as big as Ruby, I can stay up late now too, see? I can stay awake till the stars come out too." Mama and Ruby didn't know her plan. It was still a secret until she was ready for telling, and it meant she could hear Mama and Ruby planning which tomorrow Ruby would go to Grandma's so Rose would know which day to hide in the scullery doorway and wait.

~

*A*head, the red disappeared into the space where the path broke into two pieces, and the red cloak went along the part of it that bent around out of sight. Rose could go faster on this part now that Ruby wouldn't see if she turned. Faster didn't work out so well, as one of Rose's untied laces wrapped itself under her boot, around the worn leather, and pulled her feet into a tangle like a fly in a spider trap. Rose's lip trembled, and she let herself lay still in the dust like a fallen pinecone dropped by a squirrel. She pushed her face into the prickle of pine needles so the prickle of her eyes would be disguised as something else. Her heart made a noise in her ears like the rumble of the kettle on the old iron stove, when it got too hot and Mama had to pour the water into the willow-pattern teapot instead. The teapot never made the same noise the kettle did. The teapot had a story on the side that Rose liked to go to sometimes, with trees dripping their branches daintily onto a bamboo bridge. A girl in a dress from a place far away knelt beside the bridge, gazing longingly at a fish that leapt from the blue-painted river as if the water from the kettle had made the teapot water too hot. Rose could kneel too. She could be that girl—calm, quiet, ready to catch a blue jumping fish. Rose pushed her hands against the soft earth, but before she could be the kneeling girl, her knees cried out a protest. *'Ouch!'* they squealed, and Rose, instead of being the kneeling girl on the teapot, rolled onto her bottom and sat like the fat buddha she'd seen in another story about Teapot Land. She hushed her knees, afraid they would shout to Ruby and bring her running along the path to find them."Shh … shh … it's okay, knees, shh …" A trickle of red snuck down her leg, sideways from a throbbing volcano of knee; 'rupting, that's what it was doing. She saw that once in a story too. Rose watched as the blood drew a path along her pale skin. *I'm red inside. It's getting out. I'm getting redder.* She used the edge of her cloak to wipe the Ruby-colored trail, smearing it into streaks of dirty scarlet.

Good thing Rose was a big girl now. She wouldn't cry, or let her knees tell her to go home to Mama and stop following Ruby. She just had to do this one time, then Mama and Ruby couldn't tell her she was too small to go into the forest without them. Just one time. She'd tried before, but she hadn't been big enough last time, and she couldn't reach to open the door. She'd tried dragging a chair, but the chair had called out to Mama, and Mama had made Rose play in her room instead. She'd waited and waited until the pencil line on the doorframe told her she was bigger, and it was right, now she could reach! So that was how she knew she was big enough now, big enough to follow Ruby.

Mama would be proud of her, when she looked and saw how big Rose had gotten big enough to be a red rose instead of a pink one—'cept Mama was busy and might not notice. Mama and the little baby were rocking in the chair in the best room, thinking Rose was playing, being "a good girl while Ruby takes Grandma her basket, such a good, big girl, my Rose." So there, Mama had said it herself—Rose was a big girl now, and look how big she was now, getting up with her poorly knees that are showing Rose how to be red and important and not just faded like a flower in the sunlight.

Around her, the forest screeched into a frenzy of alarm and became as scary as Mama had thought it might be but Rose never believed was true. The space in between the branches and the sky was full of birds, squawking and yelling, and the trees had nothing to say, because, if they couldn't whisper, they wouldn't use their voices at all. Rose stood as still as the statue she had been when she was standing in the nook between the pantry and the scullery and wondered if the sky was falling. A girl's scream shook the birds into decision, and they left the forest, leaving gaps for the blue sky to get back in. Rose—big, brave Rose—ran to where the loudest noise had come from, although her knees tried to tell her again, "Run home, Rose. You are only pink," and around the bend in the path—a flash of grey, a flash of red, and no more noise after that.

~

Her sister wasn't there, not waiting, not walking to Grandma's, not anywhere. Her cloak lay on the dirt track, a basket spilling its contents over the path like a broken shelf in a grocery store. The path was scuffed and worn out like a footprint bigger than Ruby's had trampled, kicked, scrambled, and fought. A branch hung broken and weeping its sap. Bracken at the side of the track slowly, tentatively, lifted its fronds one by one, bit by bit, to see if whatever was there was gone or if it should stay flattened for a longer while. A red ribbon, caught, fluttered free and drifted to the ground. A part of the path was brown, sticky, like the trees had cried some more. Rose didn't look at that bit again. Rose—big, strong, getting redder Rose—knew what to do. Slowly, carefully, not rushing or clumsy like a small pink girl, she gathered the spilled apples, the bread, the bottle of Ruby-colored wine—the pinkish one had broken, the Rose-colored liquid pooling in shards of glass, glinting in the sun like a wolf's eyes caught in a flashlight's beam. Rose carefully, gently, like the big girl she was, stacked the broken glass into a neat pile of shiny jewels to catch the sunlight where it fell onto the edge of the path through the gap in the branches above. A drop of blood welled on her thumb, but she pressed it hard against the pink of her cloak until the pain spread into the fabric and faded like pink. When her pile was made, the goodies back in the basket, and most of the bracken fronds were upright again, watching, nodding in encouragement, Rose slipped from her pink cloak, folded it neatly—the blood patches facing upwards to remind her she was turning red—and placed it in the basket on top of the bread. She picked Ruby's discarded cloak from the path, shook off the debris of the forest, and wrapped it around herself.

It wasn't far now.

She left the basket on Grandma's doorstep and removed the folded pink cloak, which she clutched in both hands. She was careful not to knock on the door or make noise that would disturb an old lady from an afternoon nap, and tiptoed away, like a mouse in a pantry. Clear of the cottage, she began to skip. She felt her stride had grown longer, her shadow taller. Her red insides still leaked to color her outside even though her knee and her thumb were not really bleeding anymore, and she knew they would say she was the big girl now.

Mama was sleeping when she got home. Rose was quiet

as a sister who would not return as she unfolded her faded pink cloak and spread it carefully, gently across the baby sleeping on Mama's chest.

"This is for you, Blanche. I'm red now," she whispered and crept from the room.

BLUE MILK JOURNAL

BY MIKE VANDEVENTER

The letter comes like a joyous greeting from a land so distant I can scarcely imagine it. It's a message from the war, from Albert.

My little sister, Shelly, runs her finger over the winged globe that contains those words. "What does 'Via Air Mail, Correo Aereo, Par Avion,' mean?"

Shelly is younger than me by over ten years, and to her, the war is something that comes on the radio every evening at six and interrupts the *Triumph the Stallion* radio drama. She has no idea how much death and pain is happening across the sea or all the efforts Albert is making to keep us safe.

"It means the letter has come a long way, from Russia, and you are keeping me from reading it. Now scoot, you have potatoes to peel for dinner, and Mother needs help feeding the chickens."

She peers up at me with eager eyes, and I know what she'll ask me: "Can I use Albert's mechanized feeder and egg collector?"

I give her a moment to squirm; Mother will likely murder me with her hatchet if she finds out, but the girl needs a victory. "Sure. Just be certain you release the coil tension when you're done. We don't know when Albert will return to tinker it together again if it gets sprung. And be careful. I never liked the look of that thing!"

I'm careful with the envelope. These letters will one day be passed to my own children—a memento of the love we share—so I keep each preserved in my journal so our children can see we persevered. Even with these wars with Russia breaking out every twenty years, our spirits won't be defeated.

*D*ear Naomi,
    I'm sorry it's been so long since I wrote. The time just gets away from me with the demands of my officers. Yet, it's also very exciting!

Yesterday I received word that our village veterans have come together to assist in harvesting. That is damn noble of them. Most of those who have returned are wounded, and yet they carry on, as we all must. I know I must do more to help preserve these lives.

Today I unleashed my 'Sand Beast'—a mechanical contraption with eighteen pairs of legs and giant dorsal sail that traps the wind and works as billows! It looks so alien, and yet, alive. It does a magnificent job of preserving the beach, each foot pounding the sand and pushing it back up the shoreline.

Of course, the officers aren't sure what to make of it or of what use it might be. One suggested we use it to sweep for landmines. He pointed out that the thirty-six feet would cover a sizable swath of ground and make it safe for the infantry to advance. It's innovative, and that's something they haven't seen enough of in years.

General St. George keeps me on hand, allows me to tinker and build my automatons, but he keeps me far from the war. He says

I'm not army material, and I agree. But there must be a way my machines can help save lives here.

Corporal Preston, my assistant, suggests I build something to deploy ahead of the troops, something that will serve as a shield that can keep pace with the infantry and allow cover for the tracked artillery. I have some ideas, but my desire is to save lives. I must admit, though with some new design ideas, I think I can make one so dominant that no one will dare to challenge the field.

So, once more into the breach, as they say! I'll give it a go and see what develops.

Please give my love to your mother and Shelly.
Your Loving Husband,
Albert.

My heart swells for that odd, little man. In my mind's eye, I can see him at his workbench, his spectacles hanging near the edge of his nose as he fits some little gear into place on a machine I can't understand. I know he'd try to explain it to me, and I can feel his warmth as I roll my eyes and pull his head to my breast so he can hear my heartbeat. It's our sign; it means I don't always understand him, but he understands my heart.

It's a good memory—a warm one that leaves me all the colder for being apart for so long. Someday this war will end, and my Albert will come home. Until that day, I'll carry on and make this house our home.

~

November 12, 2027
It's been months since a letter arrived from the war. I pen a new one for him weekly. I know my letters brighten his day, even if he doesn't have time to write in

return. Sometimes it's hard to stay upbeat for him, but I do my best.

There is a lot to tell, so the writing isn't difficult. The government came to take their share of our milk and eggs, and we have the rest to sell. On top of that, we get beans, oats, and beef from a can. It's not the most appetizing thing, but it makes an acceptable stew. The real prize is the lard and flour, which I think we get due to Albert's efforts. Milk will be an issue; I can stretch it further by adding water, but it gives it a blue hue around the edges, which is a shame, as it has a sunny yellow of heavy cream that would be perfect for butter.

General St. George is a national hero, but everyone around here is very proud of Albert. In the paper are pictures of massive airships with fishlike-shaped pectoral sails that flow in the wind current. It carries enough weapons to destroy a village like ours in seconds. The newspaper credits General St. George for the weapons, but we all see Albert's hand in these marvels.

"It's from Albert!" Shelly squeals, and, for a moment, the old, vibrant Shelly is back as she races to give me the envelope. The workload has taken its toll on the girl; she should be in school learning her numbers, but we need her here. Guilt is just one more emotion to set aside until after the war.

"I'll read it aloud, but keep working. There is a lot to do before dinner."

Dear Naomi,
When creating machines, I feel I am a station above my peers. I can devise a machine to push forward a mile-long wire barrier using only wind power, hoses, and some zip ties. I concocted a machine I call a Vickers War Engine, which towers

twenty-five feet in the air, and moves quicker than a train, but it seems I am a failure as a soldier.

Corporal Preston fusses about me, his hands all over my combat kit, saying things like, "Who put your load bearing equipment together?" Then he moves the bayonet from the left side to the right and puts my canteen where the bayonet used to be. It's only a matter of seconds later, and he has my brodie off and turns it around before putting it right back on my head. "Even your helmet is the wrong way around. How did ya survive the academy, sir?"

I can't even take offense. The boy truly is perplexed.

"I wanted to save lives, so I—" I say, but Preston is back at my gear, yammering on about, "Sir, where did you get a Mills Bomb, and why is it attached to your kit by the pull ring?"

I don't even know what a Mills Bomb is or how I got one. Preston tucked it into his dusty service pouch, and even his worn, dusty thing is a testament to how little I am actually involved in the war day to day. My gear is all clean, the brass shined with pride. I suppose that is why I requested to go to the front as the Vickers goes into action for the first time. I pray the sight of it sends the enemy running. I never wanted to make machines of death.

I love you, my dear Naomi, and what I do, I do for our troops, our country, but mostly for you, my love.

Your Loving Husband,

Albert

My mother and sister sit silently, peeling potatoes and cutting green beans from our garden for dinner. There isn't much to say. Albert will truly be in the war; he's going to the front.

~

*J*anuary 13, 2028

Thank the gods Shelly is alive. Last night, she went to the chicken coop to feed and gather eggs, but she forgot to release the tension on the coils of Albert's contraption, and the mechanism sprung. Shelly was cut seriously on her left leg, and, for a time, we feared for her life after all the blood she lost.

The doctors have told us she'll be okay, but we'll have to be attentive to her injury. Medicine is short here, and everyone is trying to trade and barter for the things they need. Albert is still considered a war hero, so people are kind to us, but I feel some resentment from them. We might all be walking the same muddy path of late winter's struggles, but they notice our path is less swampy.

Despite the trials and injuries, we are doing okay. The government has imposed strict quotas on how much milk we produce, and, if we cannot make it, there is a real chance we won't be allowed to keep the old cows. They tell us the government farms are producing at a higher rate.

We've seen several dairy farms lose their cows this fall. We had to reduce our own share of the milk and cream, but I have taken to putting even more water in her milk to extend the supply; it's shamefully pale. Shelly says she cannot taste the difference, but I sure can. I suppose we all must make accommodations.

*F*eb 14, 2028

The box arrives without notice, a steamer chest with big block letters that reads, *Lieutenant. Martindale, Albert Jefferson FIRST ARMY ENGINEERS*, and my heart nearly stops. Why would his trunk be sent home? Is he okay? Is he to follow?

"Mrs., I don't have any information about this here box. I just picked it up at the train and brought it like I was told."

Dramatic as always, Mother grabs a hatchet and strides to the chest like it offends her.

"Mrs., what's your mom doing with that hatchet?"

"It's just for the security lock. My husband won't mind, just please take another look for a letter. This chest arriving is very upsetting." I take his hand in my own and try my best to implore him with my eyes.

But he is watching the crazy woman with the axe.

"Please?"

Hesitantly, he agrees and rummages through his sack.

Mother is already bashing the lock off the chest, and once liberated, she digs into it. After a moment, she fishes out a notepad. "It's his clothes and a letter from Albert." Her face looks stricken as she adds, "It's unfinished."

"Yes, Mrs., I do have another letter. It's from the War Department, I fear."

Those words crush my hope. "The War Department?" I try to say, but it comes out as a squeak, and my mother rushes to hold me up. The War Department letter could only mean one thing. "Albert—"

"No, girl. Let's read the letters and see what's what." Mother tries to reignite hope, but the wick in my chest is cold and smoking. The War Department doesn't send letters of friendship.

Mother surveys the letter, but my eyes are on the notepad and the last words my husband wrote to me before whatever befell him. Suddenly, I am desperate to know what the letter says, so I snatch it from her and tilt it into the light of day to read the words. There must be something there, some words I can find faith in.

. . .

Dear Naomi,

I'm sorry it's been so long since my last missive. The war, as always, keeps me busy, and, if not for that, I think I would have been mental by now. Some of the things I have seen, the things my machines have done, haunt me.

Even now as Preston once more straightens me out, I look over this broken, little town and grieve. Along the road are piles of bricks —scorched, ruined. I can even see a child's shoe, once black and shiny, laying shrivelled and burned. I hope there is a child somewhere with one shoe rather than a corpse who doesn't need one.

The Vickers Mark II stands proudly in what's left of the square. Its right arm is a massive Lewis Machine Rifle with rotating magazines that spits out fifteen rounds of 100-calibre bullets every second. My machines cut down anything that got in its way. Our victory is complete, and yet all I can think about is Shelly's leg. Is she okay? Has she healed up?

I should be more focused. A counterforce is approaching us from the Balkans—

I find no hope in the letter, less in the War Department's heartfelt thanks for the service of the now-missing Lieutenant Albert Martindale.

~

March 27, 2028

They took Shelly's leg last night. We cleaned it every day and night. We used some traditional forest remedies, but the infection spread. The doctor says there was little to be done. The soldiers have used up most of the medicine, so it was either the leg or her life. I held her down while they cut it off. I held her as I cried until morning.

I'm failing them all. Mother says that with spring comes hope, but I don't see a spring in my future. My future is milking cows, gathering eggs, doing anything I can to keep us going until the government takes our livestock. Can I do this alone?

~

May 5, 2028
I have not stopped crying for days now. Mother says I should be bone dry by now, but the tears of joy flow over the smallest of things, because the most unexpected has happened. Albert has returned from the war.

We were sowing the spring crops, and once more, the local veterans arrived to assist us. It seemed like there was a lot of them for some reason, and they appeared a little too jolly. For a while, I had the notion they had been into the sour mash, but then they came.

It started as a slow flow of people walking, then more and more until a wave of them were working their way through the village toward our farm. I was stunned by the amount of walking wounded, those in cars, and on stretchers, as if all the wounded were coming home at once.

It was Shelly who noticed the devices—bicycles with no peddles, people walking on mechanical legs, and holding the reigns of horses with mechanical arms. "Naomi!" she cried, "it's Albert's work! They all have Albert's machines."

My knees weakened, and before I knew it, I was knee deep in mud with tears streaming down my face. It was like a small piece of my beloved was moving before me as a hallmark of the difference he made, and people were all smiling and waving to me. At some point, the veterans lined up and were saluting—some with fake arms—as people passed, but I could do nothing but softly sob and watch them through tear-filled eyes.

"It's quite the sight, isn't it?" a familiar male voice softly breathed against my ear.

Even as my body jerked with suppressed sobs, I knew Albert was home.

"Come love, up off the ground. You'll make the boys all blubbery as they pass." He lifted me easily, and at once, I knew the strength came from an arm stronger than it should be. He was one of those wounded vets returning, but he was home and holding me, and all the weight and fear melted off in a strange mixture of laughter and tears.

I lay my head against his chest and watched the soldiers pass. My family was once more together if not whole, but missing parts and all, we are together.

LIVING COLOURS

BY ANDREW PARKER

I looked at my dull world, longing for something bright in it. Not dull as in uninteresting or boring. No, there was plenty of interest to catch the whole world's attention. The dullness was literal. A world that heretofore had been decorated with a multitude of colours, now stood monochrome. All black, white, and every shade of grey—not one speck of colour to be found anywhere.

We had no idea what was happening or why until it had progressed over a couple of months. It started with gamma rays, shortly followed by x-rays. They simply ceased to exist, at least on Earth. Space-borne telescopes still detected them from cosmic sources, but, as soon as they entered the atmosphere, they disappeared.

The progression didn't stop. Soon ultraviolet disappeared. At first, there was a celebration. No more sunburn. Then vitamin D deficiency became widespread.

The visible spectrum went just weeks ago. It became noticeable when the purples were gone and the sky paled out. Initially, there were still some blues; though, as it and greens disappeared, the sky was left only with reds. We imagined it was what it would have been like to be on Mars. When the reds went, we were left with our grey world. It got cooler, and the plants died.

I knew that soon, infrared heaters would fail, then our microwaves and cell phones. At the last, radio and television. Every living thing would die, and we had no idea what was causing it.

It weighed heavily on me. Great hopes had been placed in me because of my expertise with the electromagnetic spectrum. I did identify what was happening, but neither I nor others were any closer to understanding how or why, much less what could be done to reverse it.

~

A woman stood in a bright room lit by a wall of windows before an easel with a large canvas. The end of a brush cavorted on a palette, creating a mix of varying shades of grey. As paint-saturated bristles touched the canvas, the brush came alive. A stroke with a flourish here, several small dabs there. The brush a ballerina, the canvas its stage. The hand holding the brush seeming to only serve the purpose of keeping it from succumbing to the effects of gravity, only serving to keep it before the canvas so it could create the masterpiece unfolding before her.

As remarkable as the dance of the brush was, the woman herself was even more so. Her clothing, like everything else in the room, complemented the monochrome of the world around her. She herself on the other hand—her skin, her eyes, her hair—each radiated the natural colours so absent from the rest of the world. She paused, waiting for the brush to tell her. The bristle end dropped downward as her hand relaxed.

"Finished," she said. A glorious smile bespoke of her

appreciation for the painting before her. Ironically, though an artist, she didn't seem phased by the dull grey world around her. She found blacks, whites, and greys quite beautiful in and of themselves. She also seemed nonplussed by the fact that she alone, among the millions in her country, was the only one with her natural colours. Well, there was that one fellow at MI5, but then his colours weren't really natural, were they?

She cleaned up after herself and sat on the veranda, beholding the sights as she sipped her tea. If it were a just a matter of the sights, it wouldn't concern her as much, though she did miss the colours. No, it was rapidly becoming a threat to the great variety of life everywhere. It was time. She grabbed her phone.

~

My phone buzzed. The screen indicated, 'Unknown Number.' I declined it. On the fourth call in as many minutes, I answered.

"Brown speaking."

"Hi, Professor Brown," an exuberant voice said. "This is Magdalena Impiam, but you can call me Maggie."

"Hi, Maggie. What can I do for you?"

"I wondered if we could meet. I've something important to share."

"I'm rather busy, Maggie."

After a pause, she said, "Dr Brown, I know what's happening."

"What do you mean?"

"I know why the colours are gone."

I felt a jolt of hope. Could it be? Could she—whoever she was—know?

"Why are they gone?"

"I think we need to meet. It's complex. I can come to your campus office."

"No, home would be better. Most of my work is being done here right now. Too many to pester me on campus. I'll send you my address."

"That's alright. I know where you live."

"When?"

She had already disconnected.

~

I put a mug of water in the microwave. It took ten minutes to heat up. The microwaves were going too. I reviewed my notes as my tea steeped. It was a hopeless exercise.

I finished the tea and went outside to wait for her. I didn't even know where she was hailing from or how long it would take. Impiam. Interesting name.

I observed my pale grey lawn surrounding darker grey tree trunks. I wandered, surveying my rose bushes. The dull grey leaves were sagging, and petals were falling off half the roses. My pride and joy, they'd all be dead soon. Dead, along with the rest of us.

I walked to the end of the sidewalk and watched the people in the park across the street. Children still exhibited some energy, but the adults looked as listless as I felt. The sun shining high above was but a disc of white in a pale, colourless sky. No warmth soaked into my skin.

I heard and felt it before I saw it. The deep rumble, the vibration through the soles of my shoes. She cruised around the corner on a big V-twin motorcycle, wearing a leather duster, riding boots, and gloves. All in black. I gasped at what else I saw.

The colours were striking. The bike tank, fenders, and

sidecovers were painted in some abstract design. Colours were bright and vivid, and the patterns gave the appearance of motion. The matching bandana kept her long hair tamed. Brown or auburn? Highlights woven into dark strands. I'd forgotten how much colour hair had.

~

People at the park stopped what they were doing. I wasn't sure if it was the bike, the colours—unlike anything left elsewhere in the world—or that she arrived like an empress. Yes, yes, people. The ruler of the world has arrived.

She turned the key, and the rumbling stopped as she leaned the bike onto its stand. The metallic ticking of the hot engine the only indication the bike had been alive just a moment ago. She smiled as she approached with a glow to her face—subtle undertones of pink and lesser of blue. Beautiful tints in a world where all the rest of us, regardless of race, shared muted, pasty, grey-toned skin.

I felt a yearning for the world as it had been a few months ago—a world with bright green grass, azure skies, and stunning sunsets.

She was clearly used to the attention, the questions.

A crowd gathered.

"How is it you have colour?"

"The bike. It's so beautiful. How?"

She lit up the questioners with her smile. "Yes, such good questions. Please let me know if you figure it out, will you?"

She started to turn from them but in an afterthought, said, "You are welcome to look, but please don't touch. That bike is my baby."

A large burly man with what would've been a grey and

white beard before the changes, said, "I'll look after it for you, miss. I've one myself."

"Oh, thank you, kind sir."

We walked toward my dull front door. She paused and caressed the petals of one of the roses.

"They used to be beautiful," I said.

"Oh, they truly are, aren't they?"

I could tell she really meant it.

I pulled a pair of clippers from a small bucket on the porch and clipped off the rose, leaving a long stem.

She blushed as I handed it to her—a flash of red hues in her cheeks.

"Oh, thank you."

Once in the house, I dug around until I found a small vase and set the rose stem in it to soak.

"Professor Brown seems so … formal," she said.

"Edward would be fine."

"Yes, Edward is a good name, but I think I'll call you Vincent. You remind me of a friend I had a long, long time ago."

I sought to keep her on topic.

"Do you know? Why your bike and bandana have colours?"

"Of course."

She didn't seem inclined to offer more.

"Maybe as relevant, do you know why nothing else does? Where, why, the colours have gone?"

"Yes, I know."

"Where did they go?"

"Nowhere."

"What? But they're gone."

"No, they're still here. They're just hiding."

She spoke with authority, yet also projected the innocence of a small child.

I sighed, knowing that understanding would be a process requiring patience.

"Why would the colours be hiding?"

"Because they're afraid, of course."

"Afraid of what?"

Her countenance changed with the question. The smile waned, and her brows furrowed.

"I'm not sure yet. They haven't told me."

"Haven't told you?"

"No, not yet."

"Do you talk to colours much?"

Her rich laughter ran around the room and through the house.

"Well, not quite like we are talking, but yes, I talk to them, and they talk to me."

I wasn't sure whether she was a genius or whether I should consider calling a mental health professional. That there was real colour to her and her bike convinced me to continue.

"How?"

"Maybe it would be easier to show you."

I suppose my face illustrated dubious to her.

She touched the rose. "You miss the colours, don't you?"

"Terribly so."

"Which ones do you miss the most? The reds, the yellows along the fence, the white ones in the side yard, or … this one? Hmm, not quite pink, not really purple. I'm not a rose aficionado but as for colour, magenta seems appropriate." She giggled. "You know, there is a watercolour paint this colour? Rose madder. It smells like roses itself."

How could she have known? Sure, the red roses were dark, and the black ones, well, they were still black, but how did she know the yellows and this one?

"I miss them all," I said.

She cupped the rose and focused on it.

I held my breath as a pink hue came through the grey, like it was coming out of hiding. It brightened, the pink taking on the unseen blue hues as it settled into the rich, gentle magenta I remembered.

"Oh …" I was speechless.

"Don't share this, unless you want news agencies surrounding your house and your sitting room full of government officials with a lot of questions you can't answer."

"How is it you aren't locked in some interrogation room yourself?"

"Oh, I was accosted by several important types."

"Important types?"

"Yes. The prime minister, the Director General of MI5, some military types, a bunch of others with black suits."

"And they let you go?"

"Sure. I convinced them."

"How'd you do that."

She got a far-off look.

I sipped at tepid tea as she shared what had happened.

~

"Ma'am, you're the only person in the world we know of who still has colour," the prime minister said.

"Do you have something against people of colour?" she asked.

Apparently, not a single one of them had a sense of humour.

"Ma'am, I don't think you know the gravity of your current situation," the director said.

"Sir, first of all, I am way too young for someone your age

to be calling ma'am. I am Maggie. Secondly, you dragged me in here like a common criminal, though I've done nothing wrong, except to look different. Thirdly, I a quite aware of the gravity of the situation. The electromagnetic spectrum, as you call it, gets sorted out, or everything on this planet dies."

"I'm sorry, Maggie, for the heavy handedness. We are just very concerned," the prime minister said.

"Thank you, Prime Minister. I'd be glad to leave you a sample of my hair and skin for you to study, if you'd like."

"Will they tell us anything?" a woman in a sharp charcoal and grey pant suit asked.

"No."

"Do you know why you have colours that no one else does?" she asked.

"Yes. I missed them and asked the colours to come out of hiding for me."

There were several groans, even more eyerolls, and a few looks of overt anger.

"Miss, I will have you locked up in solitary confinement if you don't start taking us seriously," the director said.

Her own patience was stretching thin. She stood, her chair rocking backward. She took long strides, heels echoing, as she walked around the table to where the director sat.

"Loud are the words of hypocrites. You want me to take you seriously, but when I offer you an explanation, you reject it out of hand."

The director scoffed and said, "You asked the colours ..." He shook his head.

She stared at him, a picture of patience and calm.

The prime minister gasped, and someone down the table let out an expletive.

The director saw everyone staring at him, eyes wide, some mouths hung open.

"What? What is it?" As the words left his mouth, he noticed his hands—not pasty and grey but with colour. Real colour.

"I'm leaving now. I'm sure you'll have your little spooks." She lifted her hands and waved her fingers, as if speaking of Halloween goblins. "Follow me. That's fine. Just make sure they leave me alone." She stomped from the room.

No one tried to stop her.

~

"So, they let you go? I'd have thought they'd want you to make all their colours come back," I said.

She giggled. "Well, I don't think they wanted to risk it."

"Why not?"

"Picture someone vomiting after just eating split pea soup."

"Yes."

"Well, that is the colour of the director general's skin now."

The spoon clinked as I stirred the mostly empty mug.

"I'll make it a point to not cross you."

She laughed and lovingly gazed at the magenta rose.

"Maggie, who … what are you?"

"I'm a mage."

"A mage? Like a witch or magician or something?"

"So many titles have such negative connotations," she said with a sigh.

I spied the rose. "I believe you. I just haven't believed in magic since I was a little boy."

"Oh, Vincent, magic is just what we call things that happen that we don't understand. Everything I do is in harmony with the laws of the universe."

"I can accept that."

It was all so contrary to my training as a scientist, but when the world was dying, time was short, and without answers, the mind would open to new possibilities.

"I invited the colours of the rose to come out. I sent my love and appreciation for them. Manifested my desire, knowing the universe would carry the message to them. They want to come back out. All of them do."

"So, as a mage, you can command animals and do things like alchemy and stuff?"

She laughed. "You're generalizing. Thinking all mages are the same would be like thinking all scientists, or all artists are the same. We have our specialties."

"And your specialty is …?"

"I am a chroma-mage. Colours, all those you can see and all those you can't, are my specialty. I work magic with colours."

We walked back toward her bike.

A larger crowd had gathered, people having called friends to come see the miracle of colours. They parted for us.

She looked up at the big man as she straddled the bike. "Thanks."

"You're welcome, miss. Perhaps we should go for a ride sometime."

"I'd love that," she said with a smile he quickly reciprocated. "I'll talk to my boyfriend about when it'd work for him too."

The big man's smile faded.

She started the big bike.

I was sure I could hear my living room window rattle with its rumble.

The crowd stood, unmoving.

She eyed the people in front of her. "Shall I run you over?" She popped the clutch, and the bike lurched forward.

People came out of their stupor and moved aside, creating a path for her.

~

The next morning, the discovery was on the news. I was watching it when a knock sounded. She had returned.

"Have you seen it?" she asked, as she crossed the threshold.

"I'm watching it right now."

We sat on the sofa and listened to the talking heads. The astronomers had discovered it some weeks ago. The phenomena was like a cloud in space—not grey, not white, not a cloud of vapours or dust. A cloud of nothingness.

It passed the edge of the asteroid field, covering two asteroids in the process. When the cloud moved on, the asteroids were gone. Yet when the area was swept with radar, they were found to still be there—just completely invisible. Scientists performed further tests. Any wavelength sent to the cloud simply ceased to exist upon contact with it—a consumer of all wavelengths. It would collide with Earth in a day.

A talking head shared his thoughts.

"We've always assumed invisibility could only be an illusion created by the bending of light. What if colour was completely removed? Not just the colours as we see them, but of all wavelengths? What if the molecular structure of an object was unchanged, but somehow all colour disappeared? Would that not create true invisibility?"

"He's a rather bright fellow," Maggie said.

"Do you know what it is?"

"Yes, it is the *echthrós tou chrómatos*—the enemy, the destroyer of colour. This is why the colours hide."

"So, what, the whole world will become invisible?"

"Yes. Not just the wavelengths humans can see. Birds and, to a lesser degree, some mammals can see UV. That will disappear too. Infrared ..."

"There won't be heat?"

"Infrared is heat, and heat puts out infrared, but they aren't always the same thing. Microwaves won't work. X-rays, telly, radio. Not that it matters. Everything will die."

"We will all die," I said, reaffirming her words.

"Yes, but that won't happen." She jumped up. "I must go. I need to prepare."

"Prepare for the end?"

She looked disappointed in me.

I felt like a scolded little boy.

"No. There won't be an end. I must prepare for war."

"Alone?"

"No. A handful of us are scattered about the Earth."

"So, a handful of you will fight this ... this thing?"

"No, we won't fight it, but we must rally the troops that will."

~

*I*t was confirmed that night. We were the centre spot, the spot where the cloud—the monster of nothingness—would come to first. It would come down, spread across all the surface of Earth then constrict to the core, devouring all wavelengths.

~

*T*he next morning, she called.

"Meet me at Optimists Park in an hour. It's time."

"Where?"

"The dome."

⁓

I ran across the large lawn toward the hill, gasping with the effort of it.

She stood on the crown of the hill. Poised. Regal.

Her leather duster was absent, a long artist's apron in its place covered in a dazzling mosaic of colours.

I assumed she'd managed to get a lot of paint all over it until I got closer and realized it was the material's pattern. A top, pants, and even shoes, were all collages of colour. Dark black and bright white designs chased through the colours, like random cracks running through a dry lakebed.

I stopped at the bottom of the hill, not wanting to interrupt.

She watched the great monster of nothingness that hung over us. We knew this would be where it would come. It was, she had said, why she was born and led to be here. The other chroma-mages would rally and send all the colours from around the world to her. She looked from the sky to me and smiled.

"Now what?"

"I'm an artist, Vincent. I shall paint the monster into oblivion."

"Like it's a canvas?"

"No. Life is my canvas, the whole world my palette. The winds are my brushes, and together, we will paint all the colours and life back into the world."

We heard a scream as the nothingness eclipsed the sun, and the light dimmed.

She raised her arms to waist level, and winds rushed in.

They whirled, coming from several directions at once. As

they increased, they took colour. Some gusts red, some blue, some green, some yellow, some violet. They chased across the trees, shrubs, and grasses, each plant adding a texture to the colours, leaving them with the appearance of great brushstrokes.

Maggie directed the colours up into the nothingness. It couldn't consume them as long as they had a place to go, but it had to be destroyed before it reached the surface and trap them.

The winds reflected off the grey ground, giving it colour for the first time in weeks. While the great winds of colour had slowed it, the monster still advanced.

Maggie muttered something into the sky and clouds, and immense coloured sponges, rushed in. She built a barrier with them, to reinforce the brushstrokes of wind. The barrier held, but it too was being forced downward.

She raised her voice, competing with the roaring winds to be heard. It was a language I didn't know, though I thought I caught snippets of Greek, Celtic, and Latin intermingled with many other strange words. I could see the fatigue as she used her magic to paint the skies with her armies of colour.

The monster continued to creep downward.

I ran up the hill, my own raspy voice panicky in the wind, saying, "The other ones, the ones I can't see ..."

"They are here. It isn't enough." Worry, doubt, started to show.

"All of them?"

"No. One is missing."

The colours in the sky had coalesced. I knew they were all there, but for whichever one Maggie said wasn't. What I could see though, was all bright yellows and oranges, with streaks of muted reds, as if the colours had sought to become fire and lava in their effort to destroy their enemy—an enemy that refused to surrender to their efforts. That continued in its stubborn downward movement.

Maggie sank to her knees.

"The other one. What about the other one?"

"The other one. So unappreciated, not even given the respect by most to be called a colour. It hides because of what people have wrongfully associated it with."

"Will it help?"

"I will try."

She raised her voice as salty drops ran over her cheeks. "*Mavro*. Oh, beloved and maligned *Mavro*. I need you. We all need you. Won't you come save your fellow colours? Won't you save us all? Please…"

A trembling occurred beneath my feet. From the bowels of the Earth itself, from the depths of crevices and cracks, from the deepest caverns, from the far depths of the seas, a blackness arose. It rose all around us, black tendrils reaching upward, joining each other above. It rolled toward the monster, monstrous itself, rolling black thunderheads. The other colours raced around and through it. Darker colours joined it, giving portions of the endless black tints of the others. It rose and ran through and among the bright, supersaturated yellows and oranges. Yellow and orange rivers ran through it. It was truly the most brilliantly beautiful, and the most devastatingly terrible thing I could have ever imagined.

The maelstrom of black, yellow, and orange pushed forcibly against the monster of nothingness, holding it, stretching around to contain it. Black tendrils rose from the earth and oceans, cumulating above, adding to the army of colour. The black consumed everything. The other colours joined it, consuming the sky, spreading downward toward the surface.

I still felt and heard the winds but saw nothing. Absolute

darkness. We waited in silence. All of us. I sensed it before I saw, the blackness dissipating. As it had come, it returned to the ground and waters as tendrils. Some, upon touching the ground, ran like a liquid into cracks and shadows. A light came from above and grew in brilliance—

the sun. Colours chased to and fro, going where they belonged. Greens seeped toward vegetation, some blues spread across the sky. Some reds and browns ran into my shirt. I'd forgotten what colour it was.

The monster was gone. People cheered. No one who witnessed it would ever fear the dark again.

Maggie mouthed, *'Thank you'*. Colour had returned to the world with a vividity and brilliance unlike before. Maggie would later explain the colours were excited to be out of hiding. They would calm down over the coming weeks.

She waved an arm from one side to the other. Colours raced up, creating a rainbow, arcing from horizon to horizon. She repeated the motion with her other hand and created another rainbow by the first, this one from white to black, with all shades of grey between. Science would never be able to explain it, but from there ever after, whenever a rainbow shone, another monochrome twin, shone with it.

Maggie extended her palm, and a tendril of black snuck from behind the apron and moved onto her palm.

It sat there, a little black cloud, like something alive.

"One more little favour?" she asked it.

She winked at me, and, while gesturing all around, said, "This piece is finished."

She pointed skyward and the black tendril shot off her finger. Others joined it as she made a motion with her finger and her black initials appeared high above.

"Shall we, Vincent?" She turned toward the side of the park where her bike was and strolled off the hill as if nothing had happened.

A group of reporters, camera people in tow, rushed and blocked her away.

"Oh, I'm not doing questions or interviews, thank you," she said.

They barraged her with questions anyway.

She was patient for a moment then raised a finger, silencing them.

"Shall I turn you all back to the lovely pasty grey you were before?"

The media made themselves scarce.

~

We walked through the park toward her ride. I looked back and noticed her initials were dispersing and fading, like a jet trail.

"Well, you and the other mages saved the world."

"No, the colours rose to the occasion. They saved the world."

I nodded.

"Now what? I never even asked you what a chroma-mage does."

"I suppose that depends on the chroma-mage. I think this one will go to her gallery."

"Gallery? What kind of gallery?"

"I paint."

"Of course. Let me guess, abstract?"

She brightened, as if I'd given her a gift.

"Why yes, that is my preference. How did you know?"

I shrugged.

"Lucky guess."

We walked up to her bike.

"We should have dinner sometime," I said.

She nodded. "That would be great. My boyfriend and I love eating out."

I smiled. "Yes, you and your boyfriend. I'd love to take both of you to dinner."

"Goodbye, Vincent, my friend," she said as she turned the key on the big bike.

"Goodbye, Maggie, my marvellous, magical mage."

As she throttled the engine and slowly released the clutch, she turned to me and yelled over the thrum of the engine, "I really don't have a boyfriend, Vincent, and dinner would be lovely!"

She pulled away, roaring down the street.

The vibration in my feet faded along with the engine's rumble. Good vibrations.

I chuckled and thought *I wonder if it's requisite for all chroma-mages to have such colourful personalities.*

BY K J LYONS

"Miss, I want my phone fixed, and I'm not getting off here until you do something. I've told you a million times, I do not want to be transferred yet again! Reset my phone, *now*!"

"Ma'am, I'm trying to explain to you the steps to do that. I can't stay on the phone while you do that," Tierna explained.

"This is ridiculous!" the customer screamed. "I will be turning you into your supervisor and canceling my phone with your service! Goodbye!"

The call went silent. Tierna laid her head on her arms. She sighed, trying not to cry as the last customer hung up, dissatisfied. The customers never listened. She had to follow the script. Disappointed customers filled her whole day. It didn't help that the new update to the cellphones messed up a ton of settings on certain phones. Her job seemed easy. Get the customers to follow the directions she sent in a text. She figured out, quickly, she was talking to the technically disadvantaged. The one job Dean allowed her to do from home was not working out. Her phone rang one last time, as the clock struck quitting time.

"Good evening, this is Tierna. How can I help you today?" She put on her work voice.

"Hi, Tierna. It's Jane."

"Hello, ma'am."

"Tierna, I have been reading your logs from your calls today. Is something going on? You had over twenty complaints."

"Seriously? They just didn't listen. I sent the link, but they didn't follow it. They said they wanted me to fix it. How am I supposed to do that?"

"You should have transferred them to tier two."

"Not on the card. The card specifically says—"

"I know what the card says," Jane snapped. "It's done. You're done. I can't deal with any more of your customers. I will send you a label for your equipment return. When your equipment is returned, you will receive your final paycheck."

"Wait, you're…" Tierna hesitated. "No! I can do better. I promise. Give me another chance. Please?"

"You've been warned before. This is the last straw. Good evening, Tierna."

Tierna yanked the cord from the wall. She collected the box from the closet and removed the packing. She tore down the equipment and placed it into the box.

Tears trickled down her cheeks as she printed the label. Dean would be upset that she lost her job, only because that pointed out her failures. He didn't care if she worked or not. In fact, he didn't want her in a fulltime job working long hours. He'd rather her be home, cleaning up after him. He expected her to be waiting on him when he walked through the door, even when he was late. His obsessiveness hadn't changed, like he promised during their engagement.

Tierna walked the package to the mailroom in the lobby of their apartment building. Dean had insisted on living in a complex with all the amenities. He wanted her comfortable, but at home. He didn't realize that being home all the time would drive a person insane.

Once back inside the apartment, she cuddled up on the couch with a bottle of wine and her favorite snack, Doritos. TCM played on the TV as she engulfed herself in a 1930's classic. After a couple glasses, nothing seemed to dry her tears. She finally called Dean.

"Dean Collinsworth," he answered.

"Dean?" she cried into the phone.

"Tierna, I'm still working."

"I need you."

"What happened?" he exasperated.

"I got fired."

"For what? I told you not to take that job, didn't I?"

"That new update on the phone messed up some of the older phones. They were not supposed to get it, but they did. Now their phones don't work. My whole day was inundated with those kinds of calls. They all screamed at me. It wasn't my fault."

"I'll take care of it. I really have to go."

"Dean, please? I need you. Can you come home? It hurts." She sobbed.

"I'll try."

"Babe…"

Dean sighed and spoke softly. "Alright. I'll be home by dinner. Okay?"

"Thank you, Dean. I love you."

"Yeah, me too."

The line silenced as Dean's name disappeared off the phone. She glowered, realizing Dean didn't care enough to console her. She curled back up on the couch, eating her Doritos.

~

The clock ticked away. It was almost 9:00 p.m. as Tierna went into the kitchen and turned off the toaster oven, putting the plate of food in the refrigerator.

Her tears had long dried up, but the hurt was still prevalent. Tierna sauntered into the bedroom, looking for pajamas. As she stared at the tidiness of the drawer, she sighed.

Dean insisted on things being a certain way. The clothes needed to be folded just as they were seen in a department store. Dean's OCD caused him to lash out when things were not up to par. He never hit Tierna, but he verbally abused her at times. Of course, like all abusive people, he apologized right after, hugging and kissing her, swearing he would never do it again.

"Why do I stay? He doesn't care to listen to me when I need something. It's always his way," Tierna spouted.

She grabbed a suitcase from the closet and filled it with clothes and personals. She had no idea where she would go, but fourteen years with this man was enough. Fourteen years of verbal abuse, uncaring, and insensitivity were enough.

After grabbing her cellphone charger and makeup, she walked to her car. She didn't drive it much. Dean wouldn't allow her to do much on her own. She went to the market once a week and to her mother's once a month. Well, tonight, she would be on her way somewhere, anywhere.

~

Tierna was about thirty minutes down the road when her phone rang. Dean's name flashed across the screen.

Dean. She sighed and pushed the speaker. "Hello?"

"Where are you? You wanted me to come home, and now you're gone? It's almost ten o'clock! My dinner is cold in the refrigerator. My pajamas are not on the bed, and the living room is a mess!"

"I'm not your maid. I'm your wife. I needed you today. You promised you'd be home by dinner."

"I'm home!"

"Dinner is usually between six and seven."

"Right. And I know this, how?"

"Maybe if you came home once in a while, you would know!"

"I work my ass off for you!"

"I never asked you to."

"How do you expect me to take care of you?"

"All I need is a husband. I don't have anything else. You don't let me do anything."

"It's not my fault you can't have children! Maybe you need to …"

Tierna bawled as her husband continued to berate her. Her heart stopped as he mentioned the one thing she was unable to give him. He always said it didn't bother him, but when they had a fight, it still came up.

Lightning lit up the sky as thunder boomed simultaneously, shaking her car. She had driven into a storm, completely oblivious to the weather forecast. The storm grew closer.

Dean's words became a sea of blah, blah, blah. She tried to concentrate on the road, but the rain pelted the windshield. A lightning strike blinded her as it hit the road before her. She swerved to miss a fallen tree branch in the street.

"Deeeeeeeean!" she screamed in terror before a jolt turned her world black.

~

*T*ierna woke up inside someone's living room. The TV blared an unfamiliar newscast.

"Rainbow Row, Tinsley Town, and Macaroon Bay are all blocked off from the main roads. Crews are out now, trying to clean any debris. The flash flooding should clear up sometime this evening. Please do not drive through large puddles. We will be right back with the forecast."

Was that a new station? Tierna thought, blinking at the bright screen, as she roused from her slumber. She glanced around the strange room, observing a shag-carpeted floor and worn furniture in what seemed to be a strange, tidy living room. It appeared she had been transported back to the seventies.

Wait, did the announcer say Rainbow Row, Tinsley Town and Macaroon Bay?

Tierna had never heard of those places.

Tierna tried to sit up, feeling a sharp pain in her head. She touched her forehead, feeling a bandage on her head. As she braced her hands on the coffee table, she tried to stand, falling back into the sunken sofa.

"I wouldn't do that if I were you," a voice spoke to her. "You hit your noggin pretty hard."

Tierna turned to find an older woman rocking while knitting what looked like a sweater. She sported a glowing circle on her forehead, a green light. Tierna gasped, her heartbeat fluttering rapidly.

"What the…" She stumbled off the sofa. "What are you? Where am I?"

"Rainbow Row."

"Where? Is that in Kansas?"

"It's Rainbow Row." The lady shrugged.

"What's that on your head?"

"My hair. What's left of it." The lady giggled. The light changed to gray.

Tierna grabbed her purse from the table and stumbled from the house. Incoherent shouts came from behind her, but Tierna didn't stop. She teetered down the sidewalk, trying to remain upright. Stopping to catch her balance, on a tree or a car, caused the walk to take forever.

Tierna finally reached the downtown area. She sat in the grass a few times to take a much-needed break. The accident must have caused a concussion or head injury. After about six blocks, she found her car outside a garage. As she approached to inspect it, a gentleman joined her.

"Is she yours?" A man with a gray glowing light on his forehead startled her.

"Yes. Is it drivable? I need to get out of here." Tierna fixated on the glowing light then noticed his oil- and dirt-covered clothes. She scrunched her nose at the smell emanating from the man. Gray must mean poor. The other lady's light turned gray as well. Maybe it had more than one meaning. She seemed to be depressed that she was getting older. The man could have felt the same.

"No. It'll take about three days to finish it. I've already ordered the parts I need. Do you have insurance?"

"Of course, I do."

"Ma'am. I need to see the card, so I can start the paperwork. I'll tell you how much it costs later. Leave me a phone number."

"My phone! Is it in the car?"

"No. It's not in the car. You didn't have it on you when the police got there."

"Police? Can they get me home?"

"No. I'm sorry. The roads are closed."

"How will I get home?"

"You can get a room at the hotel. You might want to rest."

She glanced across the street. The houses, businesses, and other buildings were all painted weird, neon colors. They looked like a rainbow, all in their respective spots on the spectrum.

"What are the colors for?" Tierna asked.

"On the houses?" the man replied.

"The houses, the buildings, your forehead?"

"Excuse me?"

"Your forehead. You have a gray light inside your forehead."

"I think you need to go rest. Why don't I drive you to the hotel?"

Tierna nodded, accepting defeat about leaving town. Something was not right about this town. No one would give her a straight answer. They all talked in riddles. All Tierna wanted was to leave town.

The man dropped her off at the hotel and offered his card. Tierna gave him her insurance information to start working on the car. She just wanted to get on the road, but she needed something to eat and a little rest. She would call her Dad to come get her. He would know where Rainbow Row was.

She shuffled to the desk and asked to use the phone.

The lady pointed at the phone on the wall.

Tierna ambled over and figured how to dial her father's number. All she got was a busy signal. The storm must have knocked down some phonelines. She would need to try a cellphone. "Ma'am. That phoneline is down. Can I use your cellphone? I had an accident. Please? I just want to go home."

"Sure." The lady behind the counter handed Tierna her phone.

Tierna redialed the number. The phone rang, but no one

answered. She couldn't even leave a message. "Thanks. Where's the nearest restaurant?"

"Through those doors and turn right. The entrance is on the right."

"Thank you."

Tierna staggered to the restaurant, holding onto the wall for support.

The hostess greeted her with a glowing gray light. She didn't smile as she took Tierna to her booth, only handed her a menu.

"Gray must be sad or tired," Tierna mumbled, perusing the menu.

All the colors must mean something. The buildings were so vibrant and lively. One would think this was a happy town full of content, annoying people. Tierna's thoughts spun with a town full of purple Barney dinosaurs, singing and dancing. She couldn't help but giggle.

At this point in the game, she didn't care what she ate. Tierna's stomach hurt from being famished. She studied the overly populated menu.

The server approached with a glowing, brown light on her head.

"What can I get you?" the girl asked, hands shaking.

"Um, coffee and orange juice, and the number three plate, bacon and toast."

"Okay. How do you want your eggs?"

"Scrambled."

The girl snatched Tierna's menu then flurried off to take an order at a different table. She seemed frazzled and nervous, stumbling through the order while trying to remember what to ask the customer. The girl bumped into another server as she turned around, getting yelled at. Brown must mean stressed out. It took her a while to bring Tierna's drinks.

Tierna grabbed her hand before she left. "Hey, take a deep breath. You're doing fine. Just slow down so you can think," Tierna suggested. The girl smiled, her dot changing a bit to a shade of green.

"Thank you. I'm new, and it's hectic because of the storm."

"Take your time. You can focus better."

"I will. Thank you." The girl strolled away with a smile.

Green must mean happiness. Figuring out the dots and their colors totally intrigued Tierna. Maybe it was the bump on her head. She enjoyed her time away from Dean. Loving him was easy. Tolerating his OCD behaviors was too much. She decided to check out the town and not sleep. Shopping and spending some of Dean's money, he said she could share, would be the best therapy. She wasn't even thinking about going home.

After breakfast, Tierna freshened up in the hotel restroom. She was thankful she put her makeup inside her large handbag. Still holding onto the wall, she made her way along the sidewalk, stopping to hold onto a tree or railing when she found one.

A group of shops lined the colorful downtown area. All the colors of the spectrum, plastered on their walls, made the shopping fun. If the colors were there to make Tierna feel better about shopping, it was working.

She popped in the first shop, not paying attention to what it was. Once inside, she gathered her thoughts. It was a maternity shop. Vibrant colors of maternity shirts and dresses filled one side of the store, while the other sported clothing for the baby. She decided to look around.

The devastating news she received ten years ago kept her from entering a shop like this. Watching pregnant mothers search for their own attire, or that of a soon-to-be newborn was exhausting. Somehow, now, things were different.

Tierna pretended to look around while she lessened the

space between her and a group of pregnant women. She longed to see the colors on their foreheads.

The first woman appeared to be about eight months pregnant. She browsed through adorable baby dresses. Her face glowed with an emotional excitement as her eyes lit up at every turn of the hanger. Sure enough, the glowing circle was pink.

Tierna smiled. Even though she wanted to please her husband and have a boy, the thought of having a little girl was her lifelong dream.

"Can I help you look for something?" The attendant approached.

"Oh, I'm looking around. For a gift."

"Let me know if I can help." The woman smiled with her brown circle. She must hate her job.

Tierna contemplated what her own color would look like, deciding on brown. "Thank you," Tierna replied.

The attendant walked away, staring at her phone.

Tierna moved to the next woman. She pretended to look at the little boy's clothes. Instead, she observed their circles. The glowing circle changed between blue to pink. She must be having twins, one of each. Tierna giggled and held up an outfit for the woman to see. "This is so adorable. I saw a dress to match over there," Tierna spoke.

The woman cocked her head and smiled, rubbing her belly. "Is it that obvious? I must look like a cow." She laughed.

"Yeah, but it's a beautiful bump," Tierna lied, jealous of the lady.

After looking a little longer, she left, heading down the sidewalk. She noticed an adorable dress hanging in the window of the next shop. Inside the store played soft, classical music. The women exuded a sophisticated demeanor as their hands pushed the hangers aside in haste.

Tierna guessed they were looking for their larger size in a design that didn't make it.

She walked around in front of the lady, finding her own dress. The lady's glowing circle was purple. Purple must mean money or stature. The lady wore a silk blouse with a tight pencil skirt, diamond jewelry, and designer sandals. Tierna found her size and headed to the dressing room to try it on.

After finding a couple of dresses and a pair of shoes, she strode to the center of town. Tierna sat on the bench for a rest. She observed dozens of people hovered around the garden area. A fountain sat in the middle with circular benches surrounding it. Flower boxes sat between the benches, leaving just enough room to get through.

She watched the mothers trying to settle their children on a bench while they ate their ice cream. They pulled their children onto the bench, politely gritting their teeth at them. Stern whispers flew from the mothers' mouths. Green, glowing circles, pinned on the children's forehead while the mother's sported the brown, stressful circle.

On the other side of the garden sat a couple snuggled together. Tierna watched the man slip a ring on her finger as he proposed to the giddy woman. The joyous tears fell as the man kissed her softly, embracing the woman. Tierna watched their circles glow a bright red, meaning love.

Tierna disappeared into the world of glowing circle observations. She had sat so long that her stomach churned. It had hurt a lot lately, mostly from stress. Now that she didn't have a job, maybe she could learn to be a stay-at-home wife and take care of Dean like he wanted. Perhaps, she would go home and stay with her mother for a while. She wasn't ready to return home just yet.

She sauntered to a mobile vendor and examined the

menu. She was so hungry she wanted to order one of each item.

"Can I help you?" the food vendor asked.

"Um, can I get the double cheeseburger with bacon and everything on it? Also, the Doritos and a Coke."

"Coming right up. I noticed you sitting over there. Are you okay? With your head bandaged and all," the gentlemen asked.

"Oh, yeah. I'm just resting and shopping. It's so lively here, with all the colors and all. I can see why it's called Rainbow Row." She ripped off the bandage.

"It's a wonderful place to live."

"Can you tell me where we are?"

"Rainbow Row."

"Right. What's it near?"

"Tinsley Town and Macaroon Bay."

"Of course. Thanks." Tierna chuckled at the vague geographical lesson. She paid for her food and found a picnic table to eat on. The tables were placed at the end of the garden. She spotted a couple behind a building, next to the garden. She watched like a voyeur as they made out.

The guy looked around nervously.

She ate her burger while watching them, trying to see their circles. The girl turned her head so he could kiss her neck, showing her red, glowing sphere. The man quickly glanced Tierna's way, showing his almost black, glowing circle. He was obviously not a good person. Chances were, he was cheating; they were hiding behind a building.

Tierna averted her gaze after he noticed her.

The man grabbed the woman's hand and walked away.

She quickly finished her food and grabbed her bags. She headed down the sidewalk, checking out the latest fashions. Deciphering the different colors occupied her mind more than shopping. She ended up with a couple more outfits before she settled on a bench on the other end of town.

This part of town didn't have the lively colors on the walls or the wide variety of glowing circles. The people on this side of town had gray, black, or brown circles. Most were dull, not glowing. The condition of the buildings and the way the people were dressed told Tierna that gray meant poor also. Being poor led to crime, which is why they sported black or brown circles.

As she sat, trying to decide her next move, a mysterious voice spoke out. "You can see them."

"Excuse me?" Tierna asked, turning toward the voice.

"The circles. Only certain people can see them. Mostly outsiders."

"Do you see them?" Tierna asked.

Tierna found an older gentleman sitting against the side of the building, his clothing tattered and worn. The man's body odor wafted in the wind, churning her stomach. She could tell he was homeless. His circle glowed a bright green.

"I do."

"Why is your circle green?"

"I'm happy."

"Why? You don't look like you have a home."

"Everywhere is my home. I work odd jobs for people to make enough money to eat. I sleep in the garden park or on someone's back lawn. I don't answer to anyone, and I don't have to worry about drama."

"Aren't you lonely?"

"Being a reader is lonely. I was you once. I sat staring at all the colors. I sat studying their behaviors. It's addicting. You can't get enough of it. You'll become me one day." The man laughed.

Tierna jumped up, forgetting her packages, and ran

toward the main road. She headed in the direction of the garage, hoping to find her car fixed.

A few blocks away, a car pulled beside her.

"Ma'am?" A woman's voice spoke through the opened window.

Tierna stopped and looked over.

"Do you need a ride?" the woman asked, gasping at something. She sported a warm smile and a soft voice, the kind of woman Tierna was comfortable around.

"Um, okay." Tierna accepted the ride, stumbling toward the car, as the dizziness reemerged. She opened the door and climbed in. The lady moved back against her door, staring at Tierna.

"Thanks for the ride. Are you okay?" Tierna asked.

"Why do you have a circle on your forehead?"

"What? I don't live here. I don't have a circle."

"Sure, you do, a pink and blue one. It's flashing back and forth."

"Um, I don't think so." Tierna laughed, reclining the seat. "How far are you going?"

"I'm going to Bettington," the lady replied.

"Good. I need to sleep. My head hurts."

The lady's voice shook as she told Tierna to settle in.

Tierna didn't waste any time falling asleep. The thought of what the lady saw on her forehead was hurtful, but she didn't dwell on it. She couldn't see anything through the scar on her forehead anyway. The lady had to be lying.

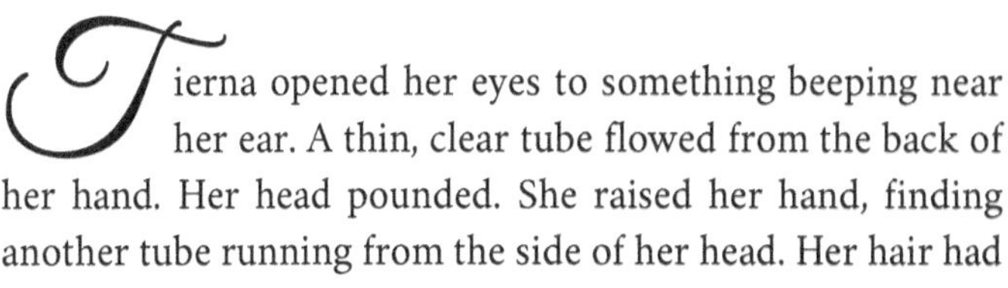

Tierna opened her eyes to something beeping near her ear. A thin, clear tube flowed from the back of her hand. Her head pounded. She raised her hand, finding another tube running from the side of her head. Her hair had been shaved in one section, and a bandage surrounded the tube. She could feel the bump on the front of her forehead. She tried to talk, but something prevented her. A tube extended from her mouth.

Tierna lay in a hospital bed. She blinked a few times, trying to make heads or tails of her surroundings. The room sported a white wall, brown cabinets, and a fuchsia-colored recliner and loveseat. Someone laid on the loveseat, covered with a blanket, sleeping. Outside the window, the sky dulled a dark shine with an illuminated ground cover from the hospital lights. Tierna shook the railing next to her arm, trying to wake the person on the couch. She tried a scream from her throat but to no avail. Nothing worked.

Tierna fumbled her hand around until she found a remote hanging on the bed railing. She pushed the red button.

A voice spoke through a speaker on the wall. "Can I help you?"

Tierna couldn't respond. Tears flowed down her cheeks. She tried to make a noise, but the tube hurt her throat to try. She repeatedly pushed the button again until someone entered the room.

"Oh! Hey, you're awake. Let me get your doctor," the nurse greeted.

The man on the couch sat upright. Dean. He ran to the bed. "Oh, Tie! Oh, my gawd, you're awake! I was so scared." Dean kissed Tierna's cheek and slumped onto the bed. He wiped her tears and smiled. "I'm so sorry. Did I cause this accident? I didn't mean to."

Tierna reached for his face, trying to dry his tear-stained cheeks. She wanted to smack him, but his eyes told a different story. He was terrified.

"You'll be okay. I know it. The doctor hasn't been back in yet. You just got out of surgery a few hours ago. They said you had a brain bleed. You bumped your head pretty hard." Dean rubbed her cheek with the back of his fingers. "I love you so much," Dean choked. "I know I haven't been there for you. When I heard you scream, I had to find you. The thought of losing you killed me. I promise I'll be a better husband. Please, don't leave me again. The last few days have been trying, to say the least."

Dean noticed a concerned look on Tierna's face. He kissed her cheek again, squeezing her hand. "Don't worry. I've been here the whole time. In fact, I told Jarrod I needed to take some time off. Especially now." He slowly rubbed her belly, smiling.

Tierna's eyes widened as she tried to talk.

The doctor entered. "Don't try. Let me remove the tube, okay? I'm Dr. Corigan." The doctor gave Tierna directions as they worked to remove the tube from her mouth.

The nurse fed her some water as the doctor sat beside the bed.

"You are one lucky lady. The paramedics said your car flipped a few times before it rested against a tree. You had a brain bleed, so we inserted a tube to drain the excess blood. We fixed the artery and patched you back up. Don't worry, your babies are fine."

"Babies?" she whispered, choking a bit. "I don't understand." Her voice cracked.

"Your twins," the doctor informed.

"Dean?" Tierna coughed, eyeing her husband.

"I know. It's a miracle. I told the doctor what your doctor told you."

"Tierna, the doctor who diagnosed you wasn't exactly wrong. Sometimes your body rectifies itself. This may be your only chance at having children. The obstetrician was in the operating room, watching the babies. They are fine. You'll be here for a while."

"Where did you find me? What about the lady who I was with?"

"Honey, you weren't with a lady. You were in your car outside the city, remember? We had a fight, and then you screamed," Dean corrected.

"Yeah. A tree fell. There was a storm."

"You're lucky the tree fell. There was a tornado up the street," Dean replied.

"What? You mean toward Rainbow Row?"

"Rainbow Row?" Dean looked puzzled.

"Yeah. The town I was in. Everyone had different colored dots on their foreheads. A lady told me I had a pink and blue one. She's the one who gave me a ride."

"Honey, you were dreaming. There's no Rainbow Row."

"This bump on my head. What color is it?"

"Well, it's bluish, and part of it is pinkish."

"What? No. The blue and pink mean boy and girl. That can't be. I really saw …"

"Your brain probably heard me tell your husband about being pregnant with twins. We discussed your injuries. Sometimes, people in a coma can hear what's happening around them," the doctor admitted.

"I'm really having two babies?" I asked.

"Yes. It's too early to tell the sex."

"It's a girl and a boy. I'm sure."

"Honey, I'll be there for you. I promise. Your parents are on their way. Your mom said she would help some. I was even thinking about moving closer to them. I could take a less demanding job or maybe go into business for myself. What do you think?"

"Oh, Dean, I love you! I didn't mean to leave. You hurt me so badly. I don't like the way you yell and make me do things."

"I know. I talked to a doctor here, a psychiatrist. I'll

continue to see him. I'll get my thoughts figured out. Just don't leave me again. I love you."

Tierna smiled and pulled Dean in for a kiss. Who knew that an accident that could have turned tragic would turn her whole life around? She was happy now. If she could see her glowing circle, it would certainly be green, with flashes of blue and pink. The storm saved her family.

SOUTHERN HOSPITALITY

BY LO POTTER

 $\mathcal{M}$ other slammed the heavy oak door on his foot as she attempted to close it. He pressed on, my mother leaning her weight into her arms to brace it shut.

"Ma'am, I do say, please take a moment to hear me through. I am happy to explain myself." The hammered brass tip of a cane appeared above the toe of his wingtip jutting across the threshold. "I hear your daughter has certain, how do we say, talents."

"Are you from the church?" Mother resisted his efforts, pushing the door and repositioning her feet.

I cocked my head as a crease materialized in the protruding polished leather.

"No, ma'am." His confidence oozed into our shaded interior, disrupting the air.

Yellowed crocheted cotton drapes shifted in this faux breeze. From the safety of my perch, the scene unfolded—my mother versus the mysterious sable shoe's owner. *Finally, one of them bothered to show. I hope Mama regrets contacting those papers now.*

"Please, ma'am. I am here on behalf of my respite home. As mentioned in my letters, I am offering myself as a benefactor to your daughter and yourself." The gravely drawl gained an edge, cutting through my mother's defenses.

She released the door. The faded calcimined oak swung into the house, creaking on its hinges, begging for oil. For a moment, her eyes widened, and her mouth dropped.

A halo of white hair and in all his traits emphasized the sunlight illuminating the man's white suit and body as a single entity.

My mother stepped backward, blinking in the blinding display.

The rawboned man welcomed himself inside with a graceful stride over our threshold.

She attempted to regain her composure, gesticulating. Gathering herself, she huffed and crossed her arms. Turning her head from the man, she shielded her eyes with her periphery. "What do you mean?"

"If you do recall, I wrote to say I am willing to pay handsomely in support of your daughter. I believe I mentioned I would foster her talents for the public benefit." He ran his fingers through his side-parted white hair and tugged his lapels to readjust his jacket's fit. "See, where I come from, we view your Josephine not as a menace but as a gift from God." His attire feigned the golden glow of health upon his etiolated exposed skin. "I have some questions I must ask to verify some details of the arrangement of course." His crocodile smile convinced my mother to uncross her arms and lead him into the front room.

Her scowl met me atop the faded vermillion velveteen wingback. "Josephine! Sit like a proper lady!"

I spun and swung my legs around then straightened my hand-me-down dress.

She faced our unexpected visitor, expanding her chest.

"So, what is your name then? How did you hear about Josephine?"

The man with skeletal cheekbones stroked his colorless beard and twisted the ends of his mustache to curl upward. His youthful yet bleached complexion betrayed his snowy top and suit. "Word gets around when you have a child with such talents. I asked around in town, and I hear her siblings do not share her unique gifts. I am sure this may have caused quite a stir, particularly among the Methodists."

Mother pinched her lips together as she motioned for the man to sit on our settee. "Yes, well …" She paused, measuring her words. "I'm sorry, I'm afraid I still don't know your name."

"Forgive me, ma'am! I thought you recognized me once you let me inside. Remember, I did write to inform you of my interest and intent to visit." He stood and knelt, taking my mother's hand. "Franklin, Harlen Franklin. It's a pleasure to meet you." He kissed her hand and returned to his seat on the settee.

With a deep exhale, she began, "It started shortly before we received notice about my Henry from the war. She was much smaller then, never having met him, barely talking." My mother motioned for me to stand as she replaced me in the chair.

"Mama, do I know this one?" I stared at the veins and bones visible through the tops of her hands, each shifting as she adjusted her posture.

"Hush, child." She turned back to the man in white. "Please forgive her, Mr. Franklin." Her muscles lost bits of definition as she breathed in the memories and exhaled the details. "Mr. Franklin, I do remember your letters. I am so sorry for the confusion. Please understand, I've dealt with many types of letters about …" Loose brown hair fell from where each twist from had been rolled and pinned with the same silver comb for all my living memory. Around the edges of her bearing, the creases of a hidden wistfulness crept in to join us. "As I was saying, Josephine was so small at the time. We'd been waiting to hear word about her father coming home from the Northern Aggression, and she looked me in the eyes and told me her pa was home. I thought this strange; she never knew him before he left! When I pressed to know what she meant, she described a man just like my Henry standing where you are sitting now. Then she waved goodbye. And it kept on happening as she could speak more."

My skin burned and pricked as she recalled the earliest details of my encounters with my father. *I don't recall a time before Pa.* Glancing about the sitting room, I remembered the days before my siblings' marriages absconded with its belongings, a time before my brother sold off anything of value, all while reminding me it was his legal right. *Pa had so much to say about his things and what to do. John Henry wanted to hear none of it.*

"Before he visited again so many times, I didn't believe her … Didn't want to believe her. I insisted she was a foolish child with no concept of the suffering she brought upon me or our family. But then we received word of his death from Virginia. Henry was one among a massacre of twenty thousand others. His death aligned with the time he first appeared to her." Mother pulled an aging cotton handkerchief with discolored spots from a concealed pocket. "I didn't want to believe my Henry was gone." She dabbed her eyes, pulling her other hand to her chest. Her pigeon-blue dress crinkled beneath the pressure of her clenched fist against her bosom.

"But around here, they say Henry wasn't the only soldier she spoke about?" Mr. Franklin leaned on his cane toward my mother.

"That's correct. She saw all the young men from our

church. That's when the rector asked us to stop attending. My sister and her husband took the rest of the children when they could. She was so little. She kept telling everyone their dead husbands and brothers were sitting in the pews with us, no less!" My mother's tears flowed in silvery streaks.

Why subject me to your sales tactics? I averted my attention to our guest and noticed the most curious thing about him; Mr. Franklin possessed the unearthly ability to maintain a ghostly shade of white. *Why am I unable to perform that degree of wash magic with our whites? How does he maintain that color?*

Mother continued, "But she was right. Admittedly, she shared only the kindest things: lovely words and thoughts—thoughts only their men would have known."

"In your solicitation to Richmond, you mentioned the trouble this has brought you and your family. Your daughter is now more than of age, but no man is interested? Again, though I mentioned it in my letter, I am so sorry."

Mother believed his sympathetic words, yet his colorless eyebrows shifted while his brown eyes scanned the barren room. Our belongings once shielded chalk-painted walls from the woodstove in winter. Now gone, these sections stood exposed. Their protected patches contrasted to the gray soot deposits and years of wear.

"Yes, and because of her … history with the church, I'm afraid every seminary I've written has informed me they were unable to accept a young woman, such as her, given to such proclivities." My mother dabbed her eyes.

I shifted the weight between my feet, accidentally attracting his attention.

His gaze crawled from my fidgeting feet upward, hovering around my waist and bosom.

I clenched my jaw, anticipating eye contact.

"May we speak alone, Mrs. Wipple? You seem weary, and dear Josephine here has been standing a long time." His toothy smile glinted with a single gold cap hidden just beyond his lip. "Now, I am sure there is something she might attend to while we discuss my proposed arrangement." His fingers flexed and curled around the carved head of his cane, the animal's head obscured from view.

"Of course." She faced me, flattening the wrinkles from the frayed caged skirts of her pigeon-blue dress. "Josephine, honey, could you see to it the washing is dry? Pull it down and fold it? Then set to harvesting whatever's ready." She waved me out of the room, her gaze remaining on our uninvited guest.

"Yes, Mama." I turned, knowing better than to argue. My mahogany braid swung and thumped against my back. Like a lone thundercloud, I stormed to the back of the house with suppressed rumbling no one could hear. There, while waiting in the back room to slip on my shoes, I stood by the door. *She'd rather me destroy our vegetable patch in this heat than hear what she has to say as they set a price for my sale.*

"There are others like her—some younger, some very close in age. They work together to help families connect with their loved ones and ease ailments brought on by the dead. As a doctor, I've spent the better part of ten years studying a unique set of phenomena. What I do has even been remarked on in Europe ..."

I let the man's voice fade behind me while I pushed beyond the threshold of the door. The August breeze licked the sweat from my skin. Marching through the remnants of our property, the yellowing grass shifted against my legs and skirts. Grumbling aloud, I hoped he could hear me. "Pa, those solicitations Mama put out worked. I bet he plans to use me as a sideshow." I grimaced and knelt to grab the wide brown grapevine basket, snarling. "I won't do that. Some of y'all were awful in life."

Nearing the twine clothesline strung between our family

oak trees, I waited. In a hot breeze, I yanked clothespins and folded the yellowing cotton sheets.

His soft baritone asked, "Jo, why such anger? What do you expect from Mary?"

"Why such anger? Why not?" I yanked a sheet off the twine, popping the pine clothespin into the air before it descended to earth with a quiet thud. "I'll always be angry! Not just at Mama but also at you! I'll never not be angry at you. You fought in a war you had no business fighting in, only to die before I was born. You died before you could learn I was Josephine Wednesday instead of Joseph Henry." I wiped away a tear from my face as I folded the sheet. "You left Mama, Ana, Sarah, and me with nothing. John Henry sold off as much as he could without ruining Mama and me. Now he's selling off the rest, including the land where generations of your family buried each other."

"Your brother is doing what is best for his dreams. He's a man now, and men must make the decisions best for them." He attempted to placate. "It doesn't matter what I think, Jo! My body is never coming home again."

"And what about what's best for me? Why can't Mama bring me with her when she heads west? Why can't John Henry stay on our family land? Why'd she advertise me to the highest bidder as an unmarried, unwanted spinster? Why sell me like chattel? What have I done besides embrace you?" I turned to find him; instead, the hot August air pulsed with bird and insect songs over the field.

"If your mother is to remarry, she can no longer live here. It's the law. Your brother doesn't want the land and needs the money. You can't stay here." His exasperated tone harkened back to childhood when he stood in our bedroom, chiding me for wrongdoings. "Your siblings moved on. Your sisters all married. Her younger sister's family has room for one more until she finds a husband. You can't hold this against her. She's tired. To remarry, she must let me go. To let this go."

A grouse jumped from a nearby tussock, disturbing a variety of other birds. The commotion brought my attention to the remnants of the back extension of the property beyond the fallow cornfields. There, our dwindling herd drank from a gurgling creek.

"But, Pa, she's heading west. I'll never see her again. And she wants to leave me with that man in there!" I returned to the faded linens and yellowed cotton. A cornflower-blue sky screeched overhead as the sounds of cicadas filled the air. Yellow rockets danced in the breeze, their bolts attracting dancing bees. I tucked my chin to hold a corner as I folded. I was forced to gaze down, and azure and violet bursts hidden on the ground garnered my attention with sullied enjoyment. Pangs of seething anger threatened my patience with Father and burned through my skin in the late summer heat. I collected details of the home I had known since birth, where generations of my family rested beneath the soil. *But inside, at this very moment, my own mother deals me away, and I don't think that man has intentions of marriage.* I shuddered, my stomach queasy. "Where will you go?" I tugged a yellow-stained handkerchief from the line as a hot breeze pulled it from my hand, and I chased it.

"Your family never actually leaves you, Jo. Of all people, you should know that best." My father's disquieted laugh echoed a red-tailed hawk in a tree nearby. "Change is only that—change. And nothing stops it. We're each simply playing a role."

I attempted to catch the handkerchief as he spoke.

"But, if you ever need reminders of where you're from, you can find them, and for signs I'm with you. Do you remember how?" His tone was soft, and the breeze calmed.

I snagged the handkerchief from the air and held it to my

nose, inhaling the smell of our herb-scented lye soap beneath the shade of a tree. The colors of the world I knew appeared darker than in the sunlight. "Tell me again." I collapsed into a seat on the tree roots and wrapped my arms and my faded embroidered dress around my knees, listening for his disembodied voice. "I'm afraid, Pa. How do I know I'm not in danger, that change won't bring something terrible?"

"Look for and save every coin you find out of place."

The warm gentle breeze brushed against my back and neck through the fabric of my dress.

"Look for the signs I'm trying to send you."

My eyes watered. *Will this be the last time I ever hear your voice?*

"Consider the actions of others before their words. People use words to lie."

"Don't leave me, Pa." I shuddered, tears streaming down my face. "I want everything to stay the same."

"Why insist on a thing like that? You hope everyone stays miserable, including you?"

A cloud passed over the sun, easing the burning August heat on my skin.

"Jo, remember, a flower blooming out of place means *I love you.* You'll always be my surprise baby girl. I came home, because I promised Mary I'd meet you."

A puffy white cloud covering the sun moved on from its perch in the sky while I sniffled back tears. "Pa?"

He was gone.

I stood and beat the back of my skirt to dislodge the golden-yellow grass seeds then returned to fold the last aged cotton sheet from the line. Carrying the grapevine basket to the house and setting it inside the back door, I eavesdropped.

"She can send you money if you so wish, or I can pay you a sort of deposit for her work in advance. It will be taken from her salary, of course, but it will allow you to be free of any responsibility as you move on in your own life."

My chest caved, and my gut twisted, the dark clouds gathering on the horizon in the sky outside reflecting my mood.

"Yes, I do think that second option may be best. My son will be selling this property too. We've barely maintained more than a vegetable patch for years now. I'm ready to move on."

I sucked my breath between my teeth, grabbed an empty wicker basket and ran to the fig tree. The green and purple droops broke off with a sticky cream sap flowing over my fingers, eating away at my skin. Their sticky sweetness smothered my nostrils. Soon my hands would crack and bleed. I pressed on, using this to block my thoughts on what little I had overheard inside the only home I'd ever known.

Moving on to the tomato plants, I grasped bunches and tore off whole sets of the plump ruby fruits. Their fuzzy green stalks braced against the poles where we had tied them as they grew. Nearby, bright green, purple, and speckled beans grew on spindling vines. These had once been my childhood summer hiding places – vines and leaves covering pitched sticks secured with layers of ancient twine. Each bean pod pulled off into my hands with pops and snaps as I turned my father's words over in my mind. *We're each playing a role.* I snarled into the wind toward the gathering purple-gray storm clouds. "I need to make my own decisions, to be my own person. I ain't some actress playing a role someone else decides. I don't want to be bought and sold!"

Moving on, I stepped into the verdant squash patch. Orange, yellow, and speckled ivory winter squash flowers opened to pollinators. Beyond the sprawling tendrils, the summer squash scattered their abundance beneath their green parasols. I twisted and ripped up the sunny-yellow squash among vibrant orange flowers and snapped dark green zucchini from their plants; their yellow flowers twisted and closed against any further visitors. I still seethed when my mother's voice penetrated my concentration.

"Josephine! Come here!"

I stood, wiping the sap and dirt from my hands on the fabric of my skirts. I rolled the phrase, *"Change is only that— change. And nothing stops it,"* around in my brain. *I don't care anymore.*

"Coming, Mama!" I shouted back. Lifting my colorful garden bounty, I did not care that harvesting under the summer heat would harm the plants I had touched. I did not care that I may never eat any of the harvest in this basket.

At the house, I set my harvest on the hand-planed table. With quiet steps, I entered the room. An unfamiliar trunk filled the floor by the man in bleached white's knees. I turned to my mother, my eyes shifting to check Mr. Franklin from my periphery.

"You'll be leaving with Mr. Harlen today, Josephine," she announced, her misty eyes hanging above rosy cheeks on her tear-stained porcelain complexion. "He'll look after you and ensure a good life for you. Better than anything I could give you."

"But, Mama …" With my gaze darting back and forth between the two, I did not want to believe it could happen this fast. My old life stood in a pigeon-blue dress with yellowing white lace, forcing me on my way. My new life stood in glaring, unnatural white with a brass-tipped cane, tapping it against the front of his shoe.

"Don't talk back to me! My decision has been made. Now, I've packed most of your things. Go to your room and check that I didn't miss anything." She clenched her jaw tight and hardened her face as I attempted to breathe on my way to the room.

On the floor, I saw a small oxidized silver coin with a hole through it. I placed it in my pocket and rummaged through my bare dressing table once shared with my sisters. Removing the side drawer, I retrieved our china-head doll. After years of neglect, her fabric body and scrap fabric dress had folded over onto herself. I opened the back of the dress and stared at the embroidered inscription along the soft, compressed body. *To Ana, Love Ma & Pa.* This relic of my eldest sister and family, this coin, and whatever my mother packed in that trunk would have to do. With change the only option, I took a deep breath and attempted to steady the heat and tears rising to my face as I returned to the front room.

"I'm ready, Mama." I lied.

~

"I dare say, you have to talk to me eventually, young lady." Mr. Franklin persisted.

Black-eyed susans dotted the yellowing grass along the road and swayed in the breeze. I crossed my arms and scooted myself closer to the side wall of the coach. On the horizon, dark clouds gathered. I prayed for torrential rain.

"Well, if you refuse to talk, you will have to listen." He drummed his fingers across the top of his cane. As he babbled, I discerned the rounded wooden top to be carved into the shape of the ugliest bald horse in existence, with large, round eyes and a drooping lower lip. Its snout, while far shorter than was proportionate for a horse, managed to possess large, flared nostrils. "Are you listening, young lady?"

I met his eyes, crossed my arms and returned to observing the landscape passing outside the window.

"As I was saying, while I am not from the area we are traveling to, you will be pleased by the climate. It's not much colder than here. Being from Mississippi myself, I was rather fond of the transition." He tapped his thumb against the top of his cane. "You do realize it will be quite dull until we get to Roanoke if you keep up this not talking business. I would rather like to get to know you, as I am sure all the other young women would."

I espied the misty green ridges of the Great Smoky Mountains cresting over the horizon.

"Miss Josephine, what can I do to convince you I am not your enemy?" He feigned speaking to himself.

I watched his transparent reflection overlap the now verdant landscape of the mountains surrounding the overland road into Virginia.

Eventually, he allowed the rocking motion and my insistent silence to conquer his attempts at conversation. The sun sank into the dimming mountains as the horses and drivers carried us toward this place he claimed to be newly named Roanoke. Once in darkness, the coach paused to light the brass lanterns on either side, jerking my starch suited companion awake.

"It appears to be nightfall, my dear. There is much less to look at outside. Perhaps we can talk now?" He preened his mustache and beard into their groomed shapes.

I sighed. "If you're so insistent, please do tell me more about this arrangement I have been conscribed to participate in." I crossed my eyes and faced him in the darkness, catching his shadowed face in the golden lantern light as it shook back and forth from the movement along the road.

"It's more an indenturement. You will join four others. We will board a train at Roanoke and eventually reach our retreat on the far side of Virginia along the James River. Occasionally, we do get called up to Philadelphia, Baltimore, or to Washington, but we spend most of our time with the guests we provide respite. We receive inquiries as far as Austin regarding our services."

As my eyes rolled, I thanked the darkness for concealment. "I don't know where Roanoke is. What services? Is this a house of ill repute?" My accusation failed to wound him.

"Oh, bless your soul, child. Heavens no. You are our guests' connection to their lost loved ones causing them great suffering. They stay with us, paying handsomely for their upkeep, of course. The real reward is they are cured of their afflictions." He chuckled in the darkness. "While you are the eldest, you are also the least dramatic of your peers, bless their hearts. The youngest, Miss Elouise, while she is a favorite among guests, she's prone to tantrums. Miss Margaret loves to sing and often connects with our guests by singing the songs their lost loved ones long to hear. Miss Rose is closest in age to you and possesses quite the gift for channeling the dead. But you ... your talents are quite extraordinary."

A pit opened above my gut and below my rib cage unrelated to the summer girdle beneath my dress. "There ain't nothing unusual about what I can do. Others simply ain't paying attention," I said with a huff, turning to stare at the now-visible full moon illuminating the landscape in monotones of bluish hues.

"It is kind of you to think so, but I must attest to the contrary, my dear." His tone indicated curled lips.

"Did my mother take the money?"

"She did. She provided me with a letter to give you upon your arrival as well." His tentative words crept into our shared darkness.

"Thank you, but I already know what it says." I sighed.

∼

*R*oanoke possessed true oddities. Hordes of people worked in bustling textile mills, and large coal engines poured thick sooty black smoke over stovepipes, filling the station with a film of grime. Miles of unfinished railroad track approached the mountains of Tennessee, promising employment for rude but strong whey-faced men with no desire for sharecropping. I tasted their bitterness as we passed them into town, their shirtless laboring bodies reddening in the sun beneath the promises of economic prosperity for a Southern industrial revolution powered by steam- and coal-powered beasts. Once in the city, no sooner had we climbed aboard this black spewing mechanical monster, the countryside flashed by faster than I had ever traveled before.

Mr. Franklin, somehow still gleaming in his blinding suit, assured me this portion of the journey required less than half the time than the trip over the mountains from Tennessee. The luxurious varnished wood interior and carmine velvet curtains with brass fixtures forged a path to excitement through my situation. I smiled at the ever-changing landscape as we rolled down from the mountains into an expansive flat farmland. We rode until the navy-blue clad conductor with shining buttons paced the aisles, announcing for the town of Suffolk.

The next coach took less time than the last. While I wilted in the August humidity, I thumbed the coin in my pocket. As the horses slowed, we approached a brick manor with several outbuildings as royal-blue water glistened in the sun beyond the greenfields in which it stood.

"Do you approve, Miss Josephine?"

My mouth agape, I blinked and shook my head. "What manner of place is this?"

"You just stated it yourself, child. This is an old manor

house. Once empty, I took the opportunity to convert it into a place of respite for the spiritually afflicted." His wide smile reflected the wooly white coats of the few grazing animals scattered about the verdant lawn as the coach rolled along the shell-coated road. At the gate, a small statue held out a lantern to welcome passersby.

Rushing down the steps to greet us were three young women. The one closest in age to myself had pinned her hair into a pleated crown, while the two younger blonde women had their hair tied up in curling ribbons. Their dresses glared a pristine angelic haze in the sun.

The smallest—somewhere early in her double digits—shouted first, running toward us. "Doc! You're home!"

As the carriage stopped, he swung open the door and lifted the youngest girl into his arms. "Yes, Elouise. And y'all have a new peer to make yourself acquainted with." His hand appeared in the doorway, his fingers motioning me forward.

I took his hand and descended to the ground, inhaling the distinct air.

The three young women smiled, the tallest among them grinning the widest.

"This is Josephine."

Attempting a curtsy, I stumbled, not yet having recovered from the extensive time in rocking, unfamiliar modes of transit.

"I'm Rose." She jutted her hand toward me. Her auburn and rust-colored hair glinted in the dappling light as it filtered through the lush tree branches. Her sapphire-blue eyes twinkled.

I took her hand, relieved.

"That's Margaret." She motioned her free hand toward the quiet dichromatic cornflower and gray-green-eyed blonde a few years our junior. Lastly, she faced Mr. Franklin. "And that's, as you've guessed, Elouise."

"It's wonderful to meet all of y'all." Waves of exhaustion engulfed me as I wobbled from the humid summer heat.

"Let's get you inside to rest. Tonight's when the fun begins." Rose winked and flashed a playful grin. She hooked her arm in mine and led me inside to what I soon learned to be our bedroom.

The room's second floor windows viewed the James River as it shimmered in the sun. I failed to recall falling asleep, but I awoke to the sun descending into night.

"Your dress is being laundered." Rose sat across the room on her own bed as she unbraided her hair, the ringlets falling loose across her shoulders and back. "I have a spare one you can wear. We are to always wear white for guests."

I blushed. "I don't own anything white like y'all do."

"Oh, that's okay! None of us did when we got here. Doc ensures we all get dresses made. Living here is the closest thing you'll ever get to being a princess." Rose pinched her mouth into a dreamy grin and glanced at the ceiling. "Besides, how else are his pure, little angels supposed to convince his guests that we're talking to their dead?"

I paused. "Aren't we?"

Rose tilted her head and blinked her long eyelashes, "Well, sometimes. But sometimes they don't say anything, and Doc says we need to give the guests something, else how will we cure their afflictions?"

I turned the oil lamp wick to light it and replaced the glass. "What exactly are these afflictions like?"

"Well, they come here grieving. Some ask about their loved ones and whether they've moved on. If they don't move on, the attachment can become painful for them. Once we discover who is attached, the spirit will fight it. Their limbs burn, their hair falls out, and one woman even started losing her sight." Rose stood to retrieve her boar-bristle brush and added a scented oil before she combed it through her hair. "After a few weeks with us, they return to normal and feel much better. Then they go home." She shrugged and returned the brush to the vanity.

Images of my mother's suffering at mentions of my father flashed through my mind. *Had I increased her suffering by refusing to let him go? Because I wanted to know him?* Her hair had never fallen out nor had she complained of pain in her limbs. Instead, she cried out for *her Henry*—my father—in the darkness when I saw him. He sat with her and attempted to hold her, sending shivers through her body with a chill only she felt. When he would ask me to tell her things, she'd beg me to stop. *She wanted to move on, not Pa.*

"How do we convince the spirits to move on?" I asked, watching Rose's face flicker in the lamplight.

"Well, that part is easy. We first need to discover which spirit is holding onto them. We try to do this on the first night. For large groups, like the one arriving tonight, we might stagger them across several nights. Tonight, we'll start with a seance after dinner. We'll start with a prayer to ask the Lord for guidance." She paused, moving one hand to her face while tapping her chin with her finger, supporting her elbow. "Follow my lead. Elouise is a natural, and Margaret will often get up to play a song. We'll do the real communicating though. The ones who want to show themselves will. Some need a bit more time."

Outside, bright yellow glints of fireflies danced across the grass to the water's edge. Somewhere in the house, several bells chimed. Rose traversed the room, plucked a dress from her bureau and tossed it to me. "Here, put this on. I'll help you finish getting ready. The guests have arrived, and we're to meet them soon. Before then, we'll need to eat in the kitchen." She retrieved a gauze veil from inside a drawer. "You might need this." She tossed it through the air.

"What will I need this for? I'm not marrying any of them."

I stared at the silky gauze draped over my hands as Rose buttoned the back of my dress.

"No, silly. It's to wear if you allow the spirit to speak through you." Rose giggled.

Dumbfounded, I lifted the gauze in front of my eyes to see how much it obscured my vision. "How is this supposed to help? Some spirits like to gesture with their hands."

Rose smoothed wrinkles from the dress's shoulders and sleeves then patted my elbows before buttoning the back. "Trust me. Not all of them will."

～

At the parlor room table sat a group of three widows in full mourning attire, an elderly gentleman, and a younger man with his mourning pin. The servants—colored men and women in the same glaring colorless attire as us—offered carafes of wine and crystal goblets to each. To the four of us, they provided crystal goblets with steaming distilled water still tepid to the touch.

Mr. Franklin entered the room, carrying his own goblet, the lamplight glinting coral through the contents of the glass. "Welcome to our humble home." He motioned to the guests around the table as they lifted their glasses for the silently circling staff to fill them. "It is with great honor that we serve you as we join in the hopes of healing our afflictions and encouraging those we have loved and cherished to move on from this world. In this sacred place, I introduce to you those pure of heart who will guide us on this journey through the veil to unroot these loved ones from where they have anchored themselves within your very souls. Let us begin with a short toast and a prayer to the Lord Almighty for blessing us with this connection to the divine. This wine has been blessed with water from the Holy Land, Jerusalem—

that same water those pure of heart will drink, but they mustn't taint themselves with the drink of sin if they are to negotiate the holy and sacred passage into Heaven for your loved ones."

I swallowed a mucus glob creeping into my throat as my stomach twisted. *I possess no divine intervention.* The others smiled and nodded, their dainty gloved hands folded neatly in their laps.

"First, let us pray. I will ask us to drink then join hands before concluding the prayer."

I squinted to see while giving the appearance of closed eyes.

While most bowed their heads, Mr. Franklin emphatically gestured. "Oh, Heavenly Father, hear us as we beg Your presence and guidance. We enter this circle to seek Your divine wisdom and prophecy. With us, we welcome Your chosen vessels. Through them, help us see our loved ones as they wait for their ascent to join You in Heaven." He paused, adjusting to a more casual tone. "Please take your glasses."

We each took hold of our cups.

"With this cup, Oh Lord, we drink to connect across the veil and to reveal ourselves to Your divine power."

Following Mr. Franklin's lead, we set down our cups after having taken a large drink.

"Then we join hands to form a circle to connect our lives together to channel Your Holy Spirit through us and give us connection. Safely guide us on this Path of Light to grant those we love freedom from the mortal realm and seek their Eternal Life in You. In Jesus' name, we pray, amen."

"Amen," most at the table repeated as I listened.

Having been banned from attending church, my heart raced with the religious references, recalling the angry responses of those we'd known. *What now?*

Elouise jumped from her chair and raced to the blonde

woman with aged streaks in her hair, her gray and black dress tailored perfectly. "Your husband. He's coming. I can sense him!" She danced about, staring at the ceiling, bounding to the elderly gentleman. "And your wife and two of your children—they're on their way as well!"

"What about my Melvin?" the eldest of the sisters asked.

Margaret rose from her chair and, in long strides, headed to a piano to play a hymn without sheet music. "This is someone in the room's favorite song," she mused aloud in a detached voice.

Rose grabbed my hand beneath the table and squeezed, giggling softly enough that only I could hear, before she stood. "Someone's young and beautiful wife is hiding. Why is she hiding?"

As I scanned the room, a little boy tugged at my sleeve to draw my attention. "Someone's son is here." I dared not seek who would respond; instead, I focused on the child before me. "What's your name?"

He touched my face and patted my cheeks with his fumbling palms.

"I think he's too young to speak but old enough to walk."

From across the table, I heard a gasp.

"Miss, say more about what he looks like," the older woman implored.

"His blond hair curls at the end, and his cheeks are round. He has a little belly and great big watery-blue eyes. He's missing the smallest finger on his right hand."

The little apparition grinned at me with six teeth.

"And he has six milk teeth."

The youngest sister sobbed onto the blonde sister's shoulder. "It's Mankin. It's my Mankin."

The little boy chewed on his left hand as he wandered to his mother and tugged on her arm to no response. He spent the remainder of the chaotic evening unphased, mesmerized by the woman who had born him—a spirit perfectly in love with his creator yet unable to interact directly.

~

The boy's affection had etched itself in my mind's eye as I drifted to sleep later. In the darkness, I asked Rose, "Will Mankin really leave his mother forever?" I clutched my china-head doll to my chest under the thin summer coverlet.

Rose sighed. "According to the doctor, the only way the Lord will choose a spirit to remanifest a body and return to improve itself is if it detaches from its former earthly bounds. For Mankin, being reborn seems pretty important, don't you think? He's a baby, and he couldn't even talk to you, right?"

I rolled toward the wall, closing my eyes for sleep. "Yes, but he shared so much with no words at all."

~

Within the day, the moans of our spectral guests failed to match those of their corporeal counterparts. Their mourning melancholy cried with open expression. All took their meals by prior arrangement, and each of us met with whomever requested our presence. The widowed sisters shared their quarters in two adjoining rooms with private access to the porch addition facing the glittering river. The eldest, Mrs. Purdey, called me to join her family to aid in their healing. Still uncertain of what had transpired the night before, I held no expectations of success.

"Is my Melvin with us now?" She shook an extended black-lace-gloved hand then patted the empty seat beside her on the pale veneered wooden bench. Her pallid complexion through the glove revealed the occasional liver spot.

I sat to join her, and she laced my fingers through hers, the rigid bones like knots in the branches of a tree. "Melvin? Mrs. Melvin Purdey misses you and loves you. Are you with us now?"

A towering man with striking sky-blue eyes stood before me. His expression pale and distressed, he knelt beside us and took the woman's free hand without her noticing. "Daisy?"

I startled, then calmed myself, focusing on the man's blue irises. "Mrs. Purdey, do you know who Daisy is?"

Her black mourning dress contrasted against his widow's bright honey-colored eyes retaining the intensity of youth.

"Only one person has ever called me Daisy, and I never …" Her brittle voice paused as she studied the flickers of sunlight emanating off the sapphire-colored James River. "Melvin, I need your blessing to move on."

The man's hand caressed her face without reaction. "I already have. But, Daisy, what are they doing to you here? Take all the money. It's yours. They're hurting you. You need to leave. It isn't safe. You need to leave. Go. Now."

Tears descended Mrs. Purdey's face.

I faced her, wondering how much she sensed her late husband's loving touch or his distressing words. Not wishing to cause the widow unease, I encouraged her, "He's mentioning something about money you may be uncertain about. He says you should take all of it. It's yours … and he wants you happy. It's all he's ever desired."

She shook her head. "What of his property? His belongings?"

The pale visage grimaced. "We take nothing with us beyond the veil, Daisy."

"All are now yours."

A flock of chickadees chirped and flew from a nearby bush.

Melvin stayed with Mrs. Purdey after she dismissed me. As I walked away, the specter remained knelt with his wife, gazing up at her and attempting to hold his hand against her face. His concern evoked a nauseous dread. *What is happening here?*

~

That evening, Mrs. Purdey's pains echoed through the walls of the great house. "I can feel his spirit departing. The great beyond is pulling him from me. It hurts!"

After receiving dinner in her room, she requested my presence.

Prior to joining her, Mr. Harlen provided me with a glass of wine, a swirling indigo tint in the red shimmering in the lamplight. *Wasn't the house wine red?*

"Take this to Mrs. Purdey and have her drink as you speak to her about Melvin. It will help soothe her into sleep." He hastened me along with the drink.

The wine stained her lips and teeth a deep violet as she drank. "Is my Melvin still here?"

The specter stood over her, a mournful expression across his face. "This is not my doing, Daisy."

"Yes, ma'am," I affirmed, holding her hand. "He's here, but only because he loves you."

Melvin nodded. "I am not the one causing this pain."

I closed my eyes and listened.

Mrs. Purdey cried out, "Melvin, it burns! My muscles ache, and there's a fire in my hands and feet from where you're letting me go. I love you, and I'll never forget you, but you must move on, and you must leave me."

Melvin pleaded and mourned, distraught by Daisy's condition. "That's not how it works, Daisy. I'm not the one doing this."

I narrowed my eyes at him and cocked my head. I mouthed to him, *Then how does it work?*

Melvin ignored me, choosing instead to focus on his Daisy. "I love you. I bring you no pain, no suffering. You've already let me go. I'm just here, just beyond, waiting for you."

My eyes widened. *Then who or what is doing this?*

As if reading my mind, Melvin turned his head toward me, his vibrant sky-blue eyes flashing as they connected with mine. "There is evil afoot in this house."

I left Melvin with Daisy's pain—two so in love and unable to experience the touch of the other. Apparently, each of the sisters felt their loved ones being torn from them within days of their arrival. Evenso, their loved ones' spirits remained in the house alongside them. Mankin played about, staring up at his mother with the same unadulterated love with the addition of confusion over her cries.

An unfamiliar specter wandered the hallways, turning corners and moving between rooms to evade contact. His brown hair was combed over a balding spot atop his head, while mutton chops graced the sides of his face. He obsessively checked a pocket watch retrieved from his shirt coat over his stout frame, clearing his throat each time.

The wine served to the guests changed after the removal process began. The moans of guests were met with a violet drink poured from a carafe kept in Mr. Harlen's office as opposed to from the barrels. While my curiosity on the nature of the spiritual ailments of Mr. Harlen's guests brewed, another, more practical question plagued my mind.

~

On the first day of September, I wandered across the yard to where a mottled gray steam condensed on the glass panes of the open windows of a small outbuilding and opened the doors. The musty, distilling steam filled my nostrils and burned my eyes. Inside, I found a dark-skinned woman stirring a steaming pot filled with fabric over an enormous woodstove. "Hello?"

Entranced in her work and humming to herself, she failed to respond.

"Pardon! Miss! How do you keep the whites from yellowing?"

The humming ceased as she faced me, shocked, then glaring. "You're not supposed to be in here, Miss Josephine. It's dangerous."

I blinked, my heart drumming up speed. "I-I understand, but could you please help me? I did the laundry for my mama, and our cotton and linen always yellowed. How do you prevent it? I never got our wash to look as white as what's here."

She pushed the fabric into the hot, steeping water with the wooden paddle as another clump of fabric floated to the surface. "We use bluing."

"You use what?" I squinted, attempting to see more details than the whites of her eyes and her striped dress in the dim light.

"You sure ask a lot of questions," she grumbled, lifting her arm to wipe sweat from her brow, and adjusted her head scarf. "We add it to the hot water to remove the yellow." She pressed the paddle again then grabbed a bottle of a pale blue transparent, shimmering liquid and added it to the boiling water. "Like this."

As we stood in the thick steamy darkness of the washhouse, a great tide of screams, agony, and anger rose from the ground below me and attached to the woman with the great wooden paddle. They reached out, joining together. The woman came into view, younger and in the cerise headscarf, surrounded by a howling force.

"I'm afraid I don't know your name. I'm sorry. What should I call you?" I teetered, attempting not to shout while stepping backward toward the only door.

These apparitions, though obscured in the dim light, gathered around the heat of the fire. Their circle of energy surrounding the woman blocked me from stepping closer. The ethereal shaking of chains echoed in my ears as the shadows undulated with waves of mourning generations attached to this young woman and towered over us both.

"My name is Israel, miss." Her mouth tight, she reigned in her voice.

"What's in bluing?" I swallowed my trembling voice, listening for anything these ghosts shared, but heard mimicry of animal sounds and languages I failed to comprehend. I fixated on the molded glass bottle as she proceeded to work. I attempted to tame the fear rising inside me.

"A blue powder gets mixed with something else before we add it to laundry. The doctor has a large jar on his desk. Now, I really need to focus on my work. Have a blessed day, miss."

I backed out of the laundry house and unintentionally slammed the door. Free of the intensity, I stared into the azure sky. The added distance released me from the generations of spirits surrounding Israel. I panted, pushing the experience from my present mind, unable to forget.

Upon leaving the laundry house, the moving air lifted the accumulated heat and sweat from my skin, cooling me to a more comfortable temperature. Sighing with relief, I turned my head toward swooshing and movement in my periphery to see Elouise bounding across the grass toward me.

"Jo! Jo! Come quick! Rose needs your help with the Northerner—that Mr. Spencer."

I quickened my pace to join her. "Why does she need my help?" I took Elouise's extended hand, and our arms swung to and fro as we approached the house.

"Something's strange with his wife," Elouise whispered behind a cupped hand before we opened the door.

Mr. Spencer—the young widower in all black with the mourning pin—sat on a plush embroidered armchair. I admired the ornate pattern of sapphire and emerald peacocks nestled amongst swirling pale pastel pink, sage, and lilac blossoms. Sitting upright, with his hands atop an opulent walking cane, his mouth remained in an unamused line.

As I passed through the archway and into view of the day room, Rose stood from her seat on the matching bench, clenching the veil in her hands.

Quickly traversing the room, she met me before I progressed farther and greeted me with the friendliest-morphed grimace she could muster. She grabbed my arm and pulled me backward into the hallway and out of his sight. "I think Mr. Spencer is lying. I don't think he's ever been married." Her panicked expression emphasized the tears cresting at the edges of her sapphire-blue eyes. "He's been berating me for the better part of the afternoon. You take a go."

Behind her, the stout man with the pocket watch cleared his throat, wandering away again.

I nodded, pressing Rose's shoulder away from the room.

Her footsteps became quieter as she gained distance down the hallway.

Gulping, I proceeded toward Mr. Spencer, his brass

mourning pin's clasped prayer hands in full display over the black silk ribbon. "Mr. Spencer, how can I help you?"

His striking, sage-green eyes met mine without a word, maintaining contact as I sat beside him. He maintained his closed mouth, and I matched our breathing, watching his every move.

He's here for a reason. I leaned forward and readjusted my seat as I waited in silence. Behind him, I detected disembodied cackles. While my gaze darted to the distraction, I regretted taking my attention from this guest.

"Do you know how Mr. Franklin obtained this property?" Mr. Spencer began.

Cocking my head, I observed this young man in his black suit, his cravat secured with a sparkling emerald and polished silver pin. "I do not, sir. As it turns out, I arrived on the same day as you."

Mr. Spencer relaxed while maintaining an unshakable and uncomfortable stare. "Let's go for a walk by the river, Miss Josephine."

I rose as instructed, accepting his proffered arm, and we strode in silence to the calming blue water.

~

The wind along the water's edge lifted my unsecured hair and the edges of my skirt, the sillage of summer blowing in from the nearby bay.

Mr. Spencer broke the silence after pausing our stride, glancing around to be assured we were alone. "My father built this estate."

I blinked and narrowed my eyes. "Your father?"

"Yes. We abandoned it before the war. My mother returned and lived here until her death, having received visions of welcoming the slaves she'd freed when we'd abandoned the property and paying them. She remarried, of course. She wrote to me often, telling me of my stepfather—a man named Harlen Franklin from Mississippi, a doctor and spiritual healer."

I listened, attempting to gather this information without blind acceptance.

"But then her letters became less frequent. She admitted to writing them in secrecy. He challenged my ownership of the property." He clenched his teeth and gripped his black kid-leather-gloved hands into fists. "She described it as burning pain, and eventually, I learned of her death."

"So, you're not here for your wife. You're here for your mother," I concluded, still processing this new information, piecing together his intentions regarding Mr. Franklin.

"I believe this doctor is a hornswoggler. I have yet to determine if the rest of you women are." He chewed on his words as he scanned the sparkling sapphire-colored waters of the James.

I closed my eyes and relaxed, having gained an improved sense of Mr. Spencer's intended connection. Opening my eyes, I saw a small woman in a pheasant hat, her face covered by a black veil, next to him with a childlike grin. "Oh, your mother is precious. Ma'am, what is your name?"

He rolled his eyes as I faced the small woman beside him, the sun sinking lower in the sky and approaching the watery horizon.

The woman in the pheasant hat laughed and spoke with a youthful orotund quality. "Florence Elizabeth Franklin. My son's name isn't Spencer. It's William Chester, like his father."

Curling my lips over my teeth to hide my own smile, I returned my attention to the green-eyed man. Measuring my words, I peered a small boat sailing along the James beyond his left ear. "Mrs. Florence Elizabeth Franklin would appreciate it if you used your father's name, Mr. Chester." As the color drained from his face, I added, "And I'd like to add she has marvelous taste in hats."

Mr. Chester had all manner of questions for his mother; many she refused to answer, instead laughing and nodding. "William, nothing can be changed now. The past is in the past."

I shook my head. "She's not providing clarity. Only pushing that nothing can be changed."

William altered his approach. "But, Mother, what did he do to you? I'd gone north to school for so long. You claimed your tea began to taste different. Then your limbs burned."

My ears pricked at this detail. *Just like the others.*

"He tried to take your father from me. I refused to comply. He told me he knew a process that would force his spirit to detach from me—to move on. I told him this was false but challenged him to try." She laughed, her bosom shaking. "You know your mother, always the one for challenging and refusing the ways any man to prevent her from having her way." She adjusted her hat, brushing the long speckled brown tail feathers of the pheasant. "First, he gave me a medicine the pharmacy manuals claimed was used for syphilis, insisting it would drive him out of me. Then he wished to use the same powder he uses in the laundry to purify me. The way he talked, it was as if talking to my husband and yellowed white linens were sins!"

I blinked as I pieced together her words. "Mr. Chester, I'll rejoin you in time. I fear there's something I must do. Please, whatever you do, don't drink anything Mr. Harlen gives you." Picking up the skirts of my dress, I rushed to the house and, with light footsteps, approached Mr. Franklin's vacant office.

On his dark, stained wooden escritoire, a large glass jar filled with a blue crystal powder glinted in the last few hours' remnants of daylight filtering through the windows. *The source of the laundry magic!* A gum label affixed to the glass claimed the contents to be Prussian Blue. *Prussian? Sounds European? How exotic!* I found an empty glass vessel on a bookshelf and used the spoon in the jar to fill the bottle. Praying the seal held, I quickly concealed it between the layers of fabric under my skirt.

Dark woods and taxidermied animals decorated the office. The inanimate animals' glass eyes aimed with permanent fixation at the front of the desk. Upon the shelf above, where I'd found the empty bottle, I saw various colored powders with names I'd never heard before. On another shelf, books on practicing medicine and the compounding of pharmaceuticals stood side by side like a wall of impenetrable mysteries. Running my hand over the labels of the bottles, I wondered what each meant by "cuprous nitrate, cuprous sulfate, potassium octacyanomolybdate, silver nitrate, thallium sulfate …" and so on.

Examining the items behind the desk closer, I noticed more unusual artifacts. The ebony stained beam contrasted with the other shelves. On it sat a silver-framed glass pane. At first glance, the silver vanity mirror appeared normal, but, as I examined it, I failed to recognize the type of mirror.

"Can I help you, Miss Josephine?"

I choked on his presence. "I was looking for you. I hoped you could educate me more about you and the history of this fine establishment I'm so fortunate to be a part of." I blinked slowly and let the hint of a smile steady my lips.

"Ah, yes, well, do take a seat, and I'd be happy to assist you in that manner." Mr. Franklin motioned to the cobalt-blue leather bench in front of the desk, its brass tacks creating a luxurious texture in the fading light. "Do excuse me while I deliver some medicine to some of our guests, and then I'll be right with you." Mr. Franklin set the carafe of wine he'd been carrying onto the side table and added a scoop of the blue powder before swirling the red wine, changing the color from a brilliant orange red to a deep violet. "I'll return shortly."

Medicine?

In the minutes of his absence, the pendulum from the clock on the office wall marked the passing moments. As my eyes tracked the back-and-forth swing, I recalled Israel and the spirits in the washhouse. While they had startled me, they did not intend to threaten me. *They're her family, like my pa ... only ... if my pa promised to meet me, why have so many generations remained for her?* I pushed the thought from my mind as Mr. Franklin reentered the room.

He sat across from me behind the desk. "Pardon the interruption." He adjusted his seat. "Now, where were we?" He placed both hands on the desk and interlaced his fingers. "Ah! Yes ... See, I fought in the war with the Mississippi Infantry and eventually traveled to Virginia with not much more to my name than a great promise that was never fulfilled. During the war, I saw a light, and God spoke to me. I was to become a spiritual doctor—more than a man of science, a man of spiritual science, curing those left behind after the war of their attachments to those needing to move on to Heaven and using His divine gifts to do His work." He smiled sweetly. "I moved into this house with my wife, a young widow named Florence, after the war. She too had seen the Light of God, and, tried as I may, it was too powerful for her. It soon possessed her fully and took her from me." He twisted and shaped the end of his beard.

"Did you two ever have any children?" I implored, feigning innocence.

He smiled. "Oh, sweet child. My late Florence had a son who moved north before I ever had a chance to meet him. I never even had an address, otherwise I would have invited him here. I requested her to write, but she explained he would never leave Boston, or New York, or wherever he was. Believing he would never return and by the right of this estate, I kept the property after she passed on." He stared out the window at Elouise and Margaret holding hands and skipping in a circle through the grass as the sheep grazed around them. "Her first husband, William, had a strong grasp on her soul. In the end, I failed to save her from the fate their bond required."

"Why did you seek us out then?" I fidgeted with my fingers then moved my hands apart to either side of my seat. The pads of my fingers slid comfortably along the dyed and stretched blue leather until they met the cool brass hardware pulling the tanned hide into the wooden frame over the internal stuffing.

"Without my Florence, I had no ability to interact with the spirits. I was only half of our Team of Light necessary to fight against the darkness taking this world. I had to find some other way to assist in the survival of the righteous against this onslaught of death and mourning clinging to this earth after the war. I knew there had to be others. She insisted there would be." Unwavering, he puffed out his chest and poised his chin with conviction.

Outside the window, birds chattered.

Say something, say something and get out of here. "Thank you for helping me understand. I truly am so honored to be part of this holy mission." I forced a smile, the bottle of powder from the jar pressed between my legs.

"I am afraid I am very busy. Is there anything else I can help you understand, my dear?" He smiled and touched the front of his gleaming waxed white hair.

"No, thank you, Mr. Franklin. You are most kind and informative." I provided a shallow curtsy.

Rushing away from Mr. Franklin's office, the bottle

gradually rolled onto the floor. As I knelt to snatch it, the plump man stood before me with his pocket watch, clearing this throat and shaking his head. Startled, I stumbled and scurried to Mr. Chester's room and rapped on the door with the back of my free hand's knuckles. "Mr. Chester?"

He cracked the door wide enough to confirm my identity before granting my entrance. "What do you have? Where did you run off to?"

I exhaled, catching my breath against the corset. "I went to Mr. Franklin's office. He has jars with powders, including this one." I put the bottle into his hand. "He called it medicine and added it to the wine of the three widowed sisters that fell so ill. It matched with something your mother said." I panted, a stitch in my side. *I miss the old corsets.*

"What did she say?" He set the bottle on a side table next to a silvery cabinet card of his mother, sadly without the hat. He took my hands and led me to a chair as I regained my breathing.

"She mentioned him giving her a treatment for syphilis. Then wanting to give her the same thing he uses in the laundry to keep the whites from yellowing to purify her soul." My head stopped spinning, and I met his green eyes as he intently listened. "I watched him add this to the wine he brought to the widows."

Over his shoulder, the bottle of blue powder accentuated against the side table's white lace tablecloth from across the room. He leaned toward me and gently pressed my hands with his thumbs. "What would my mother have me do? Help us?"

As if summoned by his words, Mrs. Franklin stood behind her son, laughing from beneath her pheasant hat. "Well, then. It's been a long time since you asked me that." Though he did not react, Mrs. Franklin wrapped her arms around her son in a passionate embrace. "I miss you so much.

I love you, my baby boy." She kissed his cheek and forehead. She returned to meet my gaze. "Well, first of all, you won't get sick, because you will start taking that medicine."

"Your mother instructs you to start taking the blue powder," I stated, ensuring she nodded as confirmation. "This will prevent you from the same fate as the others."

"What else?" Mr. Chester nodded, listening intently.

Mrs. Franklin smirked, raising her hand to her chin. "I'm not quite sure what Harlen will do if he doesn't get his expected result. He thinks he's a gift from God, and that's simply not the case. That's why he brings in his young women, such as myself."

Mr. Chester nudged my hand. "What is my mother saying?"

"That your stepfather thinks more highly of himself than what he is."

The specter doubled over, laughing.

~

"Mr. Spencer, you're doing well." While the three widows' decline had no longer progressed, Mr. Franklin noted the youngest member of the guests had entered the dining room, and he took his seat with ease. A placid expression set upon his face with the hints of healthy rouge.

"Why, yes. Miss Josephine has drawn out secrets my late wife kept hidden from me regarding your son and estate. I am at ease, it seems." He took a long drink of wine and cut into the thick slab of cured ham—a regional specialty.

"Has she now? By chance, what was your wife's name?" Mr. Franklin's eyes twinkled.

Elsewhere in the home, the sisters complained of losing their hair while their skin burned. They took their meals in their rooms. Even the elderly man of the party took his meals in his room and fared worse than the young Mr. Spencer.

"Fleur Mae—I did love her so. She was not unlike Miss Josephine or any of the other young women. She always spoke of seeing spirits, but I never believed her. She dragged us to these seances, and I saw all the best actresses across New York and around Lake Champlain and Superior."

Margaret's and Rose's eyes burned my skin while Elouise turned scarlet and scowled.

"But my wife wasn't an actress, and neither are the young women here. They're truly gifted by the grace of God. I have now spoken with her through Miss Josephine."

Elouise released a long, slow exhale while Rose and Margaret averted their attention to our guest.

"Before she passed on, she told me the only way I could ever speak to her was to find another young woman like she had been. Only, she warned me she would never reveal herself to those she knew to be dishonest with their abilities."

It was Rose's turn to scowl, her hand pinching my leg through my skirt.

Mr. Franklin sipped his wine and nibbled a bit of food. "Well, I dare say it is rather marvelous you found such a veritable example of purity and the Light of God in our Miss Josephine here."

"It is. In fact, I'd say she's a pure soul so powerful that my wife released me of all attachment immediately." Mr. Spencer grinned, narrowing his eyes as Mr. Franklin raised an eyebrow. "I believe she knows the secret of purifying souls, and we must alert all evangelical congregations across Dixie. You should take her into the world and share her with the masses!"

My eyes widened, and the warmth drained from my face, a chill taking my fingers and toes, though it was a warm September night.

His mother stood in the corner, laughing and throwing back her head as she transformed into a radiant woman wearing an emerald-green dress and a pheasant hat. This spirit sauntered over and stood behind her Mr. Chester. She winked at me, blew a kiss and touched the tip of a gloved finger to her chin.

"I would like to apologize for the falsehoods I have insisted Miss Josephine keep. My name is William Chester. I believe you may remember me from my letters?"

Both men now stood and laughed as I watched in abject horror. The two peacocks strutted alongside the table with Fleur Mae Chester—or was her name Franklin—by their side as they shook hands.

"It's good to finally meet you, sir! Do not worry yourself about this ruse; it was all out of necessity, hence my including the cabinet card of my late wife in my last post to you. I would be most interested in hearing more about your experiences with the Northern Spiritualists and their detachment from God. Let's adjourn to my study so we can talk privately. We can have our meals relocated there."

Mr. Franklin and Mr. Chester departed the dining room, their merry voices echoing in the hallways.

The smirking Mrs. Chester followed behind in her emerald, green dress.

From the hallway, I overheard his order, "Israel, please be a dear and ask the help in the kitchen to bring mine and Mr. Spencer's plates to my study. We'll be dining there this evening."

"Yes, sir." Her cerise hair covering flashed above a wicker basket of folded brilliant white linens as she passed the dining room on her way through the hallway toward the kitchen.

The spirits can lie to me. My cheeks burned and pricked as heat rose from my peers' eyes. A lump in my throat threatened what little food sat in my stomach. *She tricked me.*

Rose, Margaret, and Elouise glowered at me with tight jaws, their oppressive glares shrinking me in my seat. We all glowed in our pure white dresses.

Elouise leapt from her chair first, frothing. "How dare you allow him to insult our honor like that! Calling us liars!" She stomped her foot. "Did you feed him such slander?"

"I-I never!" I exclaimed, dizzy and overwhelmed.

"Did his wife truly reveal herself to you for that reason? Did she say those things?" Rose's lips pursed, hands clenched.

"No! She looked different. Her hat was the same, but she looked like the late Mrs. Franklin! She transformed in this very room behind Mr. Chester! I knew he lied about his name because he told me. But he lied! He swore Mr. Franklin was his stepfather and this estate rightfully his!" I scrambled for words, running out of breath.

Margaret tapped her fingers then crossed two on her left hand and flicked them. She stood, and an elegance quieted the room as she crossed to behind my chair. Closing her dichromatic eyes, she lifted her hands. "I needn't carry anger; ain't the rest of you got to neither."

"Margaret, mind your grammar!" Rose clapped her hand upon the white lace tablecloth.

"Grammar ain't important when we're being duped." Margaret spun to Rose then snapped at Elouise as she started to stand on her chair. "Sit your lily arse down and be quiet, you!"

My mind reeled. Never had the musical Margaret spoken so much in my presence. While I did not reject a junior peer taking such initiative, I did not expect the graceful dancing pianist to contain a crowd-consuming fire.

"Now, if this Mr. Chester and his wife—or whoever she is —plans to play a game, we can play too. Remember, as long as we promise to be honest with each other, that spooky falsehood-spouting, shapeshifting church bell ain't gonna mess with us."

"So, what do we do? I don't want nothing to do with any churches." I trembled, leaning on the back of my chair, gripping the sides. I gazed into Margaret's dichromatic eyes, her blond hair tied with pearlescent-silk curling ribbons, rows of bows atop her head.

"We present our different strengths of the psychic sense. Even you and Rose are not the same, clearly."

Rose started to speak, silencing when Margaret raised her open palms to the room, motioning to the calmer, youngest peer.

"I don't hear the spirits or see them, but I can tell you all about the movement of energies across the veil when we summon them." Elouise smiled, perking up at her contribution.

"I can sense when a spirit is present before it has manifested." Rose nodded, her arms crossed. "Then I can see them … sometimes. They can speak through me only if my senses are clouded." She trained her eyes away from me.

"I only see and hear spirits present, but … I don't understand more than that." I gazed into my open palms, and interlaced my fingers. I sighed, tears blinding my vision. "I'm so sorry."

Margaret laid a hand upon my back, her eyes watering as she sung, *"Then carry me back to Tennessee, back where I long to be, among the fields of yellow corn, to my darling Ellie Rhee."*

I tore the room apart with my eyes, searching for him. *Pa?*

"I can't hear him singing anymore." Rose stopped.

The others exchanged glances then gazed at their own hands in laps. In silence, we sat together.

"Your pa was old." Elouise broke the silence.

Behind her, the man with mutton chops wandered into

the room, tapping on his pocket watch before returning it to his waistcoat pocket.

"Rose! Do you see him?" I whispered, grabbing her reluctant hand.

"He's the previous owner of the house."

I stared as he milled about the room, refusing eye contact.

"He never speaks," she murmured, pulling away her hand.

Mr. Franklin reentered the dining room as the portly spirit passed through him, sauntering into the hallway. "Well, has everyone finished their dinner? Let us turn in for the night." He smiled, clapping his hands together with a swish of his palms.

~

Staring at the ceiling in my nightgown, I whispered to Rose, "If we're promising full honesty, Mr. Franklin is not."

"I know." Rose sighed.

"You know?"

"Things he says don't make a lick of sense. Spiritual attachments causing demonic-like painful afflictions?" Rose rolled over.

"I think he embellishes the truth with his science."

The moonlight cast a cool, watery glow across the ceiling through the glass panes.

"Whatever do you mean?" Her coverlet rustled as she pulled it over her shoulders with a yawn.

"In his office are jars of things he calls medicines he gives to the guests. I'm not sure he's so much as curing them as making them think they're being cured. I don't understand it yet." I inhaled deeply, closing my eyes and stretching my toes.

"That colored girl has a bottle filled by him often. What's

in that anyway? Does it have anything to do with all this?" Rose murmured, her words quieter as she fell into a sleep.

"It's bluing. It's how the house keeps all the fabrics pure white." As I thought of Israel, I recalled her army of generations upon generations of spirits joining together, surrounding her, chanting in languages I failed to understand. Her riveting brown eyes appeared in my mind, peering through my mental darkness. "It's made from a blue powder in his office. Mr. Franklin puts it in the wine after the guests fall ill. Mr. Chester used it to never get sick."

But Rose snored softly, fast asleep.

In the coming days, the widows and elderly widower recovered and departed along with their ethereal counterparts, though we confirmed nothing of their continued presence. I hoped the best for Mankin and Melvin. Mr. Chester and his wife, however, remained. Her pheasant hat and laugh haunted Mr. Franklin's office, the parlor, and Mr. Chester's quarters in her various forms as we monitored and reported signs of her presence to each other. Our anxieties grew with each day, anticipating the unknowable change approaching.

In our white dresses, we joined together, stealing moments from the observations of our watchers, biding our time as October approached. As the leaves faded with the waning days, I remembered my father's words: *Change is only that—change. And nothing stops it.* I owed it to those I could trust to embrace them through it.

PRIVILEGE AND BLUE MELANCHOLY

BY ALAINE GREYSON

Olivia Palmer meandered through the garden of blood-red tulips and peacock-blue peonies. She tucked a wisp of honey-colored hair behind her ear and surveyed the yard. White tables with slatted folding chairs littered the freshly cut grass. Men dressed in white suits and khaki fedoras complemented their female counterparts, making inane conversation and pretending to be amused. Olivia huffed. Why women were content being a showpiece instead of an equal contributor, she would never understand. Perhaps that thought prevented her from securing a match. That, or her penchant for daydreaming and troublemaking. Her mother would say it was the latter.

She lingered at the edge of the yard, observing her sisters and mother flitting about and entertaining guests. An image of another time infiltrated her mind—a time where duty and marriage were far away problems.

A group of young girls breezed past, carrying flowers picked from Lila Palmer's prized collection.

Once, Olivia and her sisters had done the same—running from the servants who tried to discipline them. A smile formed as Olivia recalled the havoc she caused—and the little boy who had taken the blame. She shook her head at the memory. It was best to focus on the present and discover a way to survive the afternoon.

Trying to conceal her existence, Olivia slunk through the crowd. If it were possible to skip this event, she would have spent the day reading in the library. Instead, she made an appearance, out of obligation and to escape the consequences. She lingered at a back table, entranced by the whistling of a violin. She glanced toward the side of the garden and smirked at the string quartet. The sweet, almost soulful music engulfed her as memories of prior garden parties danced in her mind. The memories of a brighter time, when she was young and without expectation, flooded, and a pout formed across her face. If only she could return to happier times. Olivia swayed to the music as it echoed her despair, sending mocking waves of melancholy through her bones and permeating her heart.

As the music faded and the quartet took a scheduled break, Olivia scanned the yard. *My parasol.* Her mother would rant if she was discovered without it. *What's a little sun, anyway? Who cares about alabaster skin?* She hiked the hem of her dress, revealing her ankles, and waltzed toward the center of the garden. Did she want to cause a scene? It would suit her. Olivia paused by a table, snatched a strawberry and stuffed it into her mouth.

As the juice trickled down her chin, a young woman about Olivia's age scampered toward her with an amused expression.

Behind her, a man followed, like a lovelorn puppy, nipping at the young women's heels.

"Olivia, don't you look fine! The blue in your dress brings out your eyes. I have no doubt you'll be the catch of the day."

"Go away, Brittany. I'm no one's catch."

Brittany motioned to the young man. "You'll need to bat them off with a stick, won't she, George?"

George shifted his feet and gazed at the ground. "Uh, yeah. Sure. Bat them off with a stick. Should I get her a stick?"

Brittany swatted him on the arm and shook her head. "Idiot." She turned toward Olivia. "Don't mind him. He's spent too many hours in the sun, planting me a new bed of fire lilies." Light shone from Brittany's eyes as she locked arms with George. "You need to find a man someday. George is no genuis but he's my man, and that's enough. Then you can get a bed of fire lilies. Or plain old roses if you'd like."

Olivia scoffed. She didn't want a man or a bed of stinky fire lilies. Why waste time with someone like George—someone who couldn't challenge her or carry on a conversation? She gazed across the lawn at the dandies dressed for success but with little inside their brains. The bleakness of her privileged life vexed her, throwing her further into misery. Olivia grabbed the hem of her pale blue dress and wandered toward the hedges lining the edge of the garden. She let go and smirked as her dress dragged on the ground, gathering dirt and burrs. Her mother would scold her if she saw, but the indiscretion created a rare burst of satisfaction inside Olivia. Her outstretched arm ran along the side of the hedge as she hummed Mozart's "Requiem in D Minor"—a strange song for a twenty-three-year-old but not for an old soul like Olivia. The sad, drawn-out notes called out, but went unanswered, like Olivia's veiled cries for help throughout her existence. No one in her world understood or cared. They lived for their own devices and desires. And Olivia was expected to fall in line and emulate them. Emulate Brittany. And marry someone like George. She'd rather the river swallow her. At the end of the row, Olivia curled her hand around a branch and squeezed. She bit her lip and jolted when the branch pricked her hand.

"Olivia, there you are." Lila Palmer marched toward the hedges, a wine glass perched in one hand. "Whatever is going on with you?"

"I needed a moment."

"A moment? Bradford Collins asked for you."

Ew. That name made her skin crawl. Bradford believed women should be ornaments on display—when they weren't producing children. He would never allow Olivia the library of books she desired. "I'm not interested."

"Not interested? You're not living here for the rest of your life. You need someone to take care of you."

"I can take care of myself."

"I don't know how, unless you work as a maid or a governess—like hell I'd allow that."

Olivia raised her free hand to her mouth and gasped. "Mother! Language."

"Language is the least of your worries. Your future is at stake. Twenty-three years old and still not married."

Olivia squeezed her eyes shut. Her mother was right. The world didn't operate the way Olivia wanted it to, and she could do little to change. And she didn't want to work as a maid or governess. She preferred to spend her time in the library, reading and learning about different countries and cultures. It proved more entertaining than her stuffy upper-class world. She would have to marry. But Bradford? Certainly, she could do better than that. "I don't care what you say. I'm not marrying Bradford Collins."

"You don't have many options. Who else would offer for a stubborn little upstart who would rather stuff her nose in a book? Reading isn't ladylike." Lila reached toward the hedge and yanked Olivia's wrist. She pulled it back with a look of disgust. "Olivia, your hand …"

Olivia glanced at her arm that had been entangled in the hedge. Scratches formed from her elbow to her wrist. Her hand streaked with bright, red blood. The hedge branch was firmly lodged in her palm. Carefully, she extracted her arm and dislodged the branch then tossed it aside like a ragdoll. "It's nothing."

"Nothing? You need medical attention. It could become infected."

Olivia sighed and wiped her hand on her dress. "It's just a scratch, Mom. Go back to your fancy garden soiree."

Lila latched onto Olivia's elbow and pulled. "You're coming to the house, and we're taking care of your wound."

"No!" Olivia's blue eyes sparkled, as if fire emanated and could strike down any opponent. She didn't need anyone's pity. She could tend to herself. After all, it was a lot of nonsense about nothing. A scowl formed across Olivia's face as she stormed toward the creek at the edge of their property. Alone, nowhere else seemed safe.

The muddy water sloshed at her feet as she stood at the swampy edge. Olivia kicked off her shoes and tore off her stockings. She threw them to the side and sunk her feet into the squishy soil, the grass and mud seeping between her toes. *Freedom.* She reveled in the thought only for it to be short lived.

"Excuse me, miss. Shouldn't you be with the crowd on the other side of the hedges?"

Olivia scowled at the intrusion. "What makes you think I belong there? Would any self-respecting southern belle be caught with her stockings off and her feet mired in mud?"

"That depends on how you judge respect. I've enjoyed a nice mud bath a time or two myself." The stranger lowered his fishing pole and sat on a tree stump beside the creek. "Besides, I know who you are."

The color faded from her cheeks. He was the boy. The

one who took the punishment when she stole her mother's flowers. Certainly, he would want revenge. Olivia's face paled as she recalled the scene—him led away by his ear. The screaming as the head gardener made him grab his ankles and proceeded to beat him with a switch.

"Don't be scared. I've lived on your property all my natural life." The man turned and nodded toward the house. "Seen you playing with your brother and sisters. Wanted to join in, but that wouldn't be *proper.*"

Olivia hated that word. Who decided what was proper anyway? "You could have joined. I wouldn't have objected." *And I wouldn't have let you take the blame.* Olivia stared at the man. Did he remember that day? If he did, he showed no sign.

"Ah, but your sisters would. And your mother. Then my parents would have been fired without reference. Privilege, my dear."

Privilege. She'd heard it before. Her parents believed that people were destined to certain classes. Where you were born, you stayed. Movement up the social ladder was frowned upon, and new money families were shunned. But weren't people just people? Olivia ran her bloodied hand through her honey-soaked hair, leaving a red streak.

The stranger's eyes bulged. "Are you okay? Your hand is bleeding."

She placed her hand in front of her face, her eyes fixated on the puncture wound. "It's nothing."

"I'm not trying to overstep, but it's not nothing." He reached for a box behind the stump and retrieved some alcohol and a bandage. "Let me clean it up. I promise I'll be gentle."

Why did everyone think she needed help? All this fuss over a small cut, it was ridiculous. "I said I'm fine." She balled her hand into a fist, then winced when a sharp pain radiated up her arm.

"You're not fine. If you want to keep that arm, let me help you."

Olivia glanced toward the gathering, then faced the creek. It would be unladylike for a man not her betrothed to touch her, let alone see her without her stockings. She chuckled. Concerned about impropriety? That wasn't like her. And her hand did throb whether she wanted to admit it publicly or not. What would it hurt? Olivia sighed and stared at the ground. "The alcohol, it won't hurt, will it?"

"It might sting, but the pain will be worse if we don't treat it."

Olivia nodded and trudged toward the stump and straddled it like a horse. She outstretched her hand as the stranger approached. "Get it over with."

"I'll try to be quick, as long as you hold still."

The stranger poured some alcohol on a piece of gauze and raised it toward Olivia's hand.

The strong odor mixed with the smell of fish and burnt wood, strangely intoxicating her senses. She flinched as he neared. What was this feeling and why did her insides tingle the closer he came?

"This will sting, but not for long." He dabbed the gauze on her palm, then wiped the blood and dirt, cleansing the wound.

Olivia winced.

His strokes were slow and gentle, unexpected.

It did sting, but like he had promised, it quickly subsided. She managed a tentative smile as his hand lingered on hers.

A wisp of black hair fell in front of his eyes.

Olivia's smile deepened at his boyish charm mixed with manly responsibility. Did he believe women should read?

"All clean. Now for the bandage. I'm wrapping it tight to

keep out the dirt. Let me know if it's too tight." He bent over and grabbed the white bandage, to unravel it.

"I remember you."

The stranger crinkled his eyes. "What do you remember?"

"I remember you spying on us while we played. I remember you sitting by this creek with your elbows resting on your knees, pouting. I remember you telling the head gardener that you picked Mom's peonies and gave them to me. And I remember the beating he gave you."

"Mighty good memory."

"It was awful wrong of me."

He snickered. "You were what, six? I was nearly ten, and it wasn't the first time a switch met my behind."

"Still …"

"Speaking of, why don't you stay still so I can finish the job?"

Olivia rolled her eyes. "Okay. But I don't understand why took the blame. You didn't have to. I deserved the beating."

"A privileged girl like yourself beat by the gardener? Unlikely."

"If you didn't think I'd get beat, why did you say anything?"

The stranger shrugged. "I saw a pretty girl and wanted to save her? From embarrassment at least."

Chivalrous behavior was expected from men in her class. Did that apply to the lower classes as well? Olivia had never considered it. "Regardless of why, I thank you."

"You're welcome. Now, let's get this bandage on, huh?"

Olivia conceded and straightened her palm. This peculiar little boy turned ruggedly handsome man confused her. He didn't behave as men of her class. But he didn't behave as she had learned men of the lower class behaved. They were supposed to be rude, dirty, and ungentlemanly. He proved nothing like that. Instead he was patient, kind, and good-natured. Plus, he smelled good. Olivia jolted. *He smelled good? Where did that come from? And since when did fish and burnt wood smell good?*

"You okay?"

She tilted her head and gazed into his deep-brown eyes. An unusual feeling developed in the pit of her stomach. Bradford made her want to wretch. But this stranger—this feeling—was unlike nothing she had experienced. She donned a smile and fluttered her eyes, like she had seen Brittany and her sisters do when they found a man attractive and straightened her arm. "So sorry. I'll be good."

He chuckled and reached for her arm. Starting at her elbow, he wound the bandage, covering the scratches. His fingers grazed her skin as the bandage neared her wrist. He grabbed her hand and held it. "This is the most important part. The wound on your hand is deeper than you realize. Every night before bed, have someone remove the bandage and apply more alcohol. Then reapply the bandage. Until a scar forms, you'll have to be diligent."

Never had a man been so close. It confused Olivia's senses. The usual melancholy that ruled her existence peeled away as he inched closer, winding the bandage around her palm. A sudden urge to kiss him overcame her. After all, he had proven his worth by rescuing her twice—once when they were kids and this. He deserved her first kiss. And when she was forced to marry Bradford Collins, she would have this memory to get her through.

The stranger smiled and squeezed her fingers. His gaze lingered on hers as he fell silent for the first time. For a few minutes, they froze, searching each other's eyes for a sign. Then he broke the gaze and turned toward the creek.

"That's it?"

"You're all bandaged up. Might as well get back to the soiree."

"Soiree? You needn't use fancy talk with me. I despise those things anyway."

"I see. Well, it could spell trouble if you linger. A high-society girl getting caught with a lowly servant would make headline news."

Olivia stood and waltzed toward him. She grazed his face with her hand, her eyes softening. "I haven't properly thanked you."

He smirked and wrapped his hand around her wrist. "You're playing with fire, miss. You and me? We don't mix."

"Why ever not? I already told you I don't like fancy parties and high-society expectations. I'd rather sit by the creek and read all day. I'll read, and you'll fish; it'll be the perfect life."

He placed an arm around her waist, his hand resting on the small of her back. "On your parents' land? Your wound has addled your senses."

"I've never been accused of being sane. I don't want to marry Bradford Collins. You're better suited for me."

"Am I? We hardly know each other."

"I know you're kind."

"It takes more than kindness to make a relationship work."

"Tell that to them." Olivia motioned toward the party. "Marriages are made to secure a place in society. Compatibility and love never come into play."

"It should. I'm flattered, but I must decline."

Olivia stomped her foot. "Why won't you give me this?"

"Give you what? Me? You don't even know my name let alone what I do on the estate. And you would never acclimate to my way of life. Besides, I'm not your escape plan."

She froze. He was right. She didn't know his name or his occupation. Didn't even know if he was married. Her cheeks reddened. Had she become so desperate to avoid marriage that she would throw herself at the first handsome man? Olivia returned to the stump and sat.

"I didn't mean to upset you." He stooped to one knee and caressed her unbandaged hand. "All my life, I've watched you grow up. All my life, I wished I could talk to you, play with you, even kiss you. But it's a dream that can't be fulfilled. You're used to wealth and comfort. I live in a small shack with wood floors and a kettle stove. I don't have a fancy house or fancy furniture. I have nothing to offer."

"Would you let me read?"

"If I had riches, I would build you a library."

Olivia smiled. "I would like that." She wondered how she had gone so many years barely realizing his existence, yet he had watched her all along. If she had known, would things be different? Probably not. "Do I get to know your name, at least?"

He latched onto her hand and pulled her close. Caressing her cheek with his hand, he whispered, "Brian."

"Brian." She placed her hands around his neck. "I like it. Before you dismiss me, I have one request. Kiss me, Brian."

"One kiss. Nothing else."He licked his lips and leaned close. Slowly, he placed a feathery kiss on her moist lips, his hands encircling her back.

Olivia melted. The sensation was new and all encompassing. This was what it felt like to be kissed. The smell of fish and burnt wood intoxicated her as the kiss deepened. If he refused to make her his, at least she would have this kiss. And the memory of the one person who defeated her blue melancholy.

THE AERIALIST

(IN SHADES OF BLUE) BY JINNY ALEXANDER

My insides feel as if I have swallowed my bag of juggling balls. They tumble inside my stomach, piling up, ready to burst through my throat. Now they stick together as a solid lump and bring tears to my eyes. This is my reaction whenever I see Bella; I yearn for her, and it hurts. She pulls my soul towards her like gravity pulls me to earth. As always, today she is center stage, star of the show, and top of the billing. And I, as always, watch her from the side, a little off center, never quite within her view but always close. I am her audience, her cheerleader, and her support. I am the first to applaud and the last to leave after every show. I am the wings to her stage. I am never certain whether she knows I'm here.

The crowd falls silent as she makes her entrance to the band's solemn march. The procession is led by a pair of dancing horses each as white as the somber face of a clown, each bedecked with a plume on their headpieces as black as the fall of the curtain as the lights go out. Next comes Bella held high on the shoulders of her supporting cast—the troupe of acrobats. The acrobats march in perfect step—

three on each side of her—to the beat of the band. Left, together. Left, together. They hold Bella firm and still in pride of place, balanced with perfect poise above them. The band falls silent, then a single trumpet proclaims her presence.

My gaze follows her, and there is silence once more. I sense in the slight shift of the air that the heads of all others in the audience also turn to track her path. We are spellbound. The horses part, one left, one right, their handlers leading them to the grass where they will graze contentedly until needed for their next part in this show. I know they are gone, although I do not see them go; I cannot tear my focus from my beautiful Arabella. The rest of the procession continues onwards towards the dais, where the acrobats lower Bella into position. Even in this total stillness, the gathered audience is enthralled by her. The silence is broken only by small sounds of awe and the uncomfortable shuffling that accompanies hard wooden benches. A muted sigh ripples from the seats behind me. I am not alone in being moved to tears by her entrance; I hear muffled sniffing from across the aisle, and I am distracted from Bella for an instant by slight movement from the couple alongside me. They surreptitiously wipe their eyes, her with a delicate handkerchief, him with the corner of his sleeve. Bella's presence is mesmerizing, and the spectators overflow with emotion.

I crane my head towards her, as does every other person here. We are drawn irresistibly towards her, as children during an interval are drawn to the line for candy floss. She is the pop to my corn. I can see her clearly now. She is dazzling. I gaze at her face, the thick stage makeup hiding her perfection and her flaws. I have watched her in her dressing room, and I know her marks and blemishes. Her smooth white skin is layered with stage paint; it hides the smattering of bronze freckles and the scar on her neck. Delicately painted swirls of shimmering blue frame her dusky lashes. I cannot see her eyes. She keeps them shut for the trickiest moves and the falls. Her unruly dark hair has been coerced into a neat chignon. The two ends of the lace bow twist through a few stray tendrils that soften her cheekbones. I yearn to brush back the curls from her face, to softly kiss the lines of her throat, but I remain unmoving, rooted to my seat, as if my legs would not hold me upright.

Bella, also frozen in place, loses the crowd's attention momentarily as the ringmaster steps to the podium. He turns to the gathering with outstretched arms. With pride and passion etched into the lines on his face, he begins his introductions. "Arabella, our outstanding aerialist …"

But the customary applause that always follows introductions drowns out his words. His speech rarely varies as he presents his star performer.

I drift in and out of listening as my focus is still with my exquisite dancer. The ringmaster's words will never be enough to describe her, and they bounce off me like raindrops: "flying with angels," "to the skies," "a heavenly being," "not of this earth.' I long to hold her down to earth, to ground her with me forever. I long to hold her, but she is out of reach.

As the ringmaster gives the address, Arabella lies unmoving, wrapped in endless yards of sky-colored silk, ready for the next cue. Today's address is tinged with sobriety; this afternoon matinee will be her last show. Poignancy hangs in the air like Bella's shadow. I imagine her shadow now, dancing in the spotlight with her, high above the enthralled onlookers as she soars through her routine in the roof space of the big top. They fly together as one, Bella and her shadow, swirling, twisting, rising, falling.

I see her again and again, night after night, show after

show. I have seen her show so many times now that I do not really see it anymore but instead see a montage of overlapping moments from many performances. I see her in my thoughts even when I am not in the big top and when she is not performing. She haunts my dreams and my daydreams. A slideshow of our own private performances runs on an endless loop through my mind, and I cannot imagine a world where I will never see her dance again. I watch her turbulent descents as the caresses of her flimsy blue ropes unravel. I feel my heart stop momentarily every time she skillfully halts her drop just inches from the sawdust-covered floor. I feel my heart jolt awake again as she untangles herself to begin each new ascent. She is a spider on a web, and I am her captivated prey. I see her suspended above me, soaring across the striped roof space—a bluebird against a red and white sky. She is swirls of blue silk. She is sequins glistening in the flashes of illicit cameras. She is grace and serenity. She is Bella, my Belle, my exquisite Arabella.

As always at her shows, people bring flowers. Now they surge towards her to lay their wilting blooms around her. They stroke her skin, touch her arms, her face, the shining fibers of her azure costume. Their tears and her sequins sparkle in the glare of the electric lights. Today, she accepts this attention with serenity and calm. Today, her usual fire is quenched. She displays no sentiment amid the emotions of her devotees. Tears flow freely now, as this, her final appearance, reaches its climax. The crowd returns to their seats, and the acrobats come forward once more to escort Bella for her grand exit. The lid is closed onto her coffin, and these six pallbearers lift her again to their shoulders. The congregation falls silent once more. Those juggling balls in my stomach have converged to obstruct my throat. They choke me. I cannot breathe. I cannot stop the performances replaying in my head. I know that slow-motion flashbacks of

Bella's last show will come unbidden and unfettered. I cannot breathe, and I cannot stop the show. Bella, my Bella, swirling, twirling. Bella, flying, gliding, rising, falling. Bella hanging, spinning. Still.

She rested there on the sawdust in a glittering lake of her silks, the fabric's colors darkening with the acrobats' tears. They cradled her head in their arms as they unwound the cascade of material from her neck. I reached silently, uselessly, towards her from my place in the shadows with my arms and my heart and my soul. The crowd, still expecting this to be anything but her swansong, had waited, frozen and silent, for their cue to applaud but were given only a final curtain as Bella's lifeless body was shrouded from view. Now, as then, she is wrapped in a cocoon of azure, a heart-wrenching parody of the tangle of cloth pooled around her as she lay dying in the circus ring.

The two white horses are brought to the church steps to lead the procession to the graveside. The acrobats resume their careful harmonized steps. Left, together. Left, together. I press my tongue to the roof of my mouth, but it is not enough, and I cannot quell my tears. My heart beats as slowly as the steady beat of the drum. I wonder if it will stop. From this walled graveyard outside the little church on the hill, I look down to the field where the big top still stands—silent, empty, flagless. Then I sink, sobbing, to my knees in the damp earth by the graveside as Bella and my heart are lowered, in blue silken ropes, for the very last time.

ABOUT THE AUTHOR

JINNY ALEXANDER

Jinny was first published in Horse and Pony magazine at the age of ten. She's striving to achieve equal accolade now she's (allegedly) a grown up.

Jinny obtained a distinction in an Open University Advanced Writing course in 2017, and since then has had some success with short story and flash competitions. Dear Isobel will be her first published novel. She also has a series of cozy mysteries in the pipeline.

Jinny teaches English as a foreign language to people all over the world. Her home for now is in rural Ireland, which she shares with her husband and a steady stream of visitors from overseas, and far too many animals. Her children are grown and almost independent now. Jinny quite likes to shut the door on all that, and write.

ABOUT THE AUTHOR

KYLEIGH MCCLOUD

North Dakota native Kyleigh McCloud lives in Minnesota with her husband and fourteen-year-old cat. Passionate to her core about writing, she attended Minnesota State University Moorhead and graduated with a BS in Mass Communications, emphasis in Print Journalism.

Kyleigh enjoys writing contemporary women's fiction, historical, and romance. She has published short stories and a debut holiday novella, *Her Mother's Last Christmas Gift*. When her head is not in the clouds, Kyleigh spends her downtime gardening, photography, reading, and spending time with her family and friends.

ABOUT THE AUTHOR

KJ LYONS

KJ Lyons writes a variety of genres, specializing in Romance Suspense. They have been writing on and off for over thirty years. The last six years have been dedicated to full time writing, leaving over seventy novels and novellas. They have three novels published and another coming out in 2021.

ABOUT THE AUTHOR

LO POTTER

Lo Potter publishes fiction, non-fiction, memoir essays, and poetic works. Previous works include contributions for The Poison Cast podcast; a memoir essay and flash fiction piece in After Alexei; and "Alexithymia in 2020", Stigma Fighters, May 17, 2020, and many works on CoffeeHouseWriters.com You can find and purchase their recently published collection of poetry "L'identité Politique." Based in the Pacific Northwest, they enjoy spending time with friends and family while searching for moments of laughter hiding in unexpected places.

ABOUT THE AUTHOR

MIKE VANDEVENTER

Mike VandeVenter is the author of the short story "Requiem for a Lyer" In the short story anthology "Piano." Having experienced the battlefield struggles and seen the effects of war on the home front, he has focused his writing on not just military science fiction from the combat side, but the experiences of those who stay behind and managed the home and family. With several writing projects ongoing, this retired Army Veteran lives in South Western Idaho in the United States, and when he isn't writing he spends as much time as he can with family, his dogs, and goats.

ABOUT THE AUTHOR

ANDREW PARKER

Andrew Parker has been writing fiction for five years, nonfiction for decades. His writings are comprised of an eclectic mix of novels, short stories, poetry, commentaries, and narratives. A discovery writer, he often finds himself surprised as the first reader of his works, as plot twists and character development unfold. A love of words and a desire to bring positive to readers motivates him to continually pound on the keyboard. Andrew's 'day job' for the past 29 years has been as a mental health and substance use treatment therapist. While he won't ever completely give that up, he hopes to shift more of his time and energy into writing. Other published stories include Shadow Angel, in Personal Bests Journal Issue 1. The short story Catacombs is scheduled to be published in September 2021.

ABOUT THE AUTHOR

ALAINE GREYSON

Alaine Greyson lives outside of Baltimore, Maryland with her husband, son and cocker spaniel puppy. She loves to push the envelope with her stories and strives to make her readers sympathize with characters from all backgrounds. Alaine is an avid reader and considers Jane Austen and Diana Gabaldon to be her literary heroes. She loves Mexican food, 80s music and is a Robert Downey Jr. super-fan. You will find mentions of things she loves throughout her books.

www.ingramcontent.com/pod-product-compliance
Lightning Source LLC
Chambersburg PA
CBHW050140110726